PANHANDLE BANDITS

PANHANDLE BANDITS

JACKSON COLE

WHEELER
CHIVERS

This Large Print edition is published by Wheeler Publishing, Waterville, Maine, USA and by BBC Audiobooks Ltd, Bath, England.
Wheeler Publishing, a part of Gale, Cengage Learning.
Copyright © 1938 by Leslie Scott.
Copyright © renewed 1966 by Leslie Scott.
The moral right of the author has been asserted.

LIBRARY OF CONGRESS CATALOGING-IN-PUBLICATION DATA

Cole, Jackson.
   Panhandle bandits / by Jackson Cole. — Large print ed.
     p. cm. — (Wheeler Publishing large print western)
   ISBN-13: 978-1-4104-2945-2 (pbk.)
   ISBN-10: 1-4104-2945-8 (pbk.)
   1. Large type books. I. Title.
PS3505.O2685P36 2010
813'.52—dc22
                                         2010017705

BRITISH LIBRARY CATALOGUING-IN-PUBLICATION DATA AVAILABLE

Published in 2010 in the U.S. by arrangement with Golden West Literary Agency.
Published in 2010 in the U.K. by arrangement with Golden West Literary Agency.

U.K. Hardcover: 978 1 408 49225 3 (Chivers Large Print)
U.K. Softcover: 978 1 408 49226 0 (Camden Large Print)

Printed in the United States of America
1 2 3 4 5 6 7 14 13 12 11 10

PANHANDLE BANDITS

CHAPTER I
NORTHWEST TERROR

The sun, reddening the western sky, bathed the vast Texas Panhandle in a bloody glow, symbolic of a tortured land, as Philip Horton pushed through the Pass. He stared eagerly at the Promised Land, the grassy, undulating plateau where the Horton sheep grazed. The herd was thin and decimated by drought and the long trip from Oklahoma, but the lush grass gave Horton the hope that his flocks might graze and wax strong again.

Tall, with the flat muscles of young manhood, he drew in a deep breath of the warm, scented air, his powerful chest expanding. His face, smoothly bronzed by healthy life, firm jaw and straight nose, clear, wide-set eyes that shone with an appealing light, made him a handsome picture of rugged power. All this was enhanced by the inherent self-possession and strength of pioneer blood that caused men years older to look up to him as a leader.

He could not guess to what lengths his flaming courage was to be tested, what terror gripped the Panhandle for hundreds of square miles. The scene looked so peaceful here —

Horton's horse jumped as a bullet shrieked a warning overhead. His strong brown hand dropped to the pistol strapped to his lean hips. His narrowed, trained blue eyes sought the rising dust cloud toward him.

Keen of vision as he was, it was impossible for him to pierce the distance and see the panorama of horror unfolding across the wild spaces, individual experiences adding to mass panic. Two hundred miles west, wild-galloping horses drew a covered wagon away from a burning shack around which whooped fierce-painted Indians. In the retreating wagon crouched a terrified woman, clasping a child to her while her blood-streaked husband drove for their lives from their newly-built home.

Smoke columns along the north and south line told that other settlers were being attacked by parties of Comanches. But Horton could see none of this, neither could he see far south, where rode grim-faced ranchers, pausing at scattered waterholes to stare

8

at piles of dead steers, as the buzzards rose up with raucous cries, disturbed at the feast.

At that moment, as Phil Horton waited for the approach of these hostile men, a thin, scrawny man dropped off a horse in a distant bush-fringed depression. The tiny man's right eye was covered by a black patch, and he sprinkled from a brown-paper sack some white powder onto salt cakes set for the cattle, then emptied the bag into the brown, quiet water of the pool.

The click of hoofs caused him to turn. A young cowboy rode over the rise to confront him.

"What yuh doin' here?" the rider demanded suspiciously. "Le'ssee that bag —"

The black patch stirred, exposing a raw eye-socket. Charlie Long, the line rider, heard a gun click behind him in the mesquite; he turned, a fatal error. The little man dropped the brown bag and his hand flashed out. Long's eyes were blinded by a viscous liquid that burned like red-hot needles. He tried to rub it out, but this only made it worse, and, doubled in agony, he fell from his saddle as his horse reared in fright.

A screech issued from Long's writhing lips. Masked men jumped from the mesquite and poured six-gun bullets into the helpless body, until Long ceased to squirm.

A huge hombre laughed harshly.

"C'mon," he ordered. "We're through on this range now, got it all covered. The Guv'nor's timed it jest right."

That vast territory had been touched off to bloody flame. From peace it was suddenly blazed into a state of war, and none knew where to turn. New homes were burned as Indians threatened; masked men rode the range, and in the towns to which terrified settlers hurried for protection, more lawless hombres skillfully added to the terror by robbery and murder, flying bullets.

In Making City, the county seat and metropolis of the north, a silver-tongued orator harangued the crowds, demanding law and order be restored, while similar meetings were held through the Panhandle.

And a lean rider, a loaded pack horse behind him, headed for Making. A shot crackled out and he rolled off his horse to crash down a steep, bush-fringed slope, lie sient as death!

Of all this Phil Horton knew nothing. Standing his ground, he only heard the peaceful musical tinkle of the bell-ewe's approach, as the old female led the flock out on the grassy flats. The woolly gray creatures spread out to graze, rangy sheep-dogs flanking them, keeping them in order.

Dave Horton, his father, strode up. He was a heavier, shorter man than his handsome son, hard-bitten, with seamed cheeks and gray-streaked hair. He seemed slow but inexorable, like the sheep he tended. Their old herder, Jefferson Smith, got down from the supply wagon to join them. He was older than his boss, a hatchet-faced fellow whose fierce loyalty shone from his frosty eyes and sunken cheeks.

"What's wrong, Phil?" Dave Horton growled.

"Cowmen, I guess," Phil replied, as another bullet whipped past and hit a sheep, the animal flipping back and lying down on its side, while those about it followed suit, impelled by herd instinct.

Jeff Smith ran back to the wagon and picked out his Sharps' buffalo gun, returning to stand at Phil's other side. Angered at the wounding of the sheep, Smith raised his weapon and it boomed like a small cannon, the great slug wooshing through the air.

The Hortons waited, staring across the plain which had the awesome sweep of a mighty sea. The spring sun had wheedled the soil to bloom and the vivid grass carpet was sprinkled with radiant flowers. It was a scene of wild grandeur, breath-snatching in size. Though the surface looked level, it was treacherously undermined by prairie dog cities, dangerous to a horse unused to such footing.

Here grew mesquite, sage, chaparral and cactus of every sort from tiny balls covered by long, gray hairs to giants fifty feet high. There were large areas without creek or waterhole, but ranging animals traveled great distances to drink. The rains of centuries had carved deep canyons, with fanciful pillars and frowning turrets. One of the cracks, made by Rabbit Ear Creek, had caused the Hortons to hunt the pass through the hills in which the stream rose, as the canyon had proved uncrossable.

The whooping cowboys, firing volleys over them, slowed at the vicious sound Jeff Smith's buffalo bullet made. The doughty sheepmen, outnumbered three to one, stood their ground, and the horsemen swept to a stop twenty-five yards from the compact Horton group. The garb of the newcomers told their occupation. They wore leather chaps and wide hats, spurred boots, colorful costume of the cow country, contrasting with the simple and duller dress of the sheepmen, who usually walked tirelessly about their monotonous work.

"Hey you," the cowboy foreman bellowed

furiously, "get them sheep offa this range 'fore we run 'em into the canyon! Yuh're stampedin' our cows jest from the smell of them woollies."

Reciprocal anger flared in Phil Horton as the hereditary enemy so rudely accosted them. "Go to hell! We've bought a lease on this country and we're going to use it! Stop that crazy gun-play, you're scarin' our sheep, but not us!"

Cowmen hated sheep, for their stock would run at the odor of them and the sheep nibbled off the grass to the roots, ruining a range for cattle. And the sheepmen returned the dislike with interest, remembering the attacks made on them by their foe.

"Wait," Dave Horton ordered as he stepped forward, "I'll talk to 'em, Phil." He walked toward the cowboys. Phil could make out the brand on their horses, a bell with a B in it, B Bell. He quickly followed his father to back him up as the fearless sheepman coolly approached. "I paid a thousand dollars for a grazin' lease here," Dave explained to the red-faced foreman. "We're from Oklahoma, the drought drove us out."

"We're drivin' yuh back," snarled the foreman. "This range is occupied, savvy? We

13

don't let sheep come south of the border."

"Who's boss round here?" demanded Dave.

"Marley Bell, of the B-in-a-Bell, President of the Panhandle Grazers Union."

"Huh! Why, I was told yuh was movin' yore cattle south, that this range was open to sheep. I know a dozen flocks headin' this way, they all bought leases from gents."

"Yeah, there's sheep come in all along the north border," the foreman said angrily. "We're turnin' 'em out, dead or alive, savvy? Some of 'em got through to the south and ruint the range 'fore we knowed they was in. Now you get!"

Though menaced by the crowd of enemies, the sheepmen were prepared to fight. Only the flick of a lash was needed to start a bloody battle. But as hands went for guns, a rider hurried in from the southwest.

Phil Horton's rage cooled as he looked at the newcomer. It was a young woman, small, daintily formed, with exquisite clear-cut features, full red lips, the sheen of sun on her coppery hair lovely as an artist's dream.

"What's wrong, Hank?" she demanded.

"Aw, Miss Lydie," the foreman replied, "these dang sheepmen're lyin' 'bout havin' leases on our range."

She faced the Hortons. Her amber eyes were very earnest, and she caught Phil's admiring glance, addressed him.

"My name is Lydie Bell, my father's Marley Bell, head of the Panhandle Grazers. Our members have had a lot of trouble with sheepmen, and there've been some fights, men wounded on both sides."

Dave grew excited. "Fights, huh? Why, I'm head of the sheepmen, Miss Bell. Reason we're late is we helped the other flocks start off, we have to travel far apart on account of not wantin' to get the critters mixed. We all bought leases from an agent in Oklahoma who told us the cowmen had decided to move south across the Canadian."

"Whoever told you that lied to you," she said. "The whole country's upset, and I don't like it. Bullets are flying, grangers are coming in and fencing off waterholes, there's trouble in several counties. The Comanches who ride the Staked Plain west of here are roused up, burning out settlers and chasing them into the towns. And poison's been spread across the Range, killed thousands of cows. There's a rumor that the sheepmen were doing it to clear the way for their sheep, and in revenge for having been driven out."

The startling news roused both Phil and

Dave Horton. The small, isolated bands of shepherds, who looked upon them as chiefs, were in deep trouble. Phil Horton could see that the fighting and terror in her home land deeply hurt the young woman.

"I don't believe our friends spread any poison, miss," Phil cried, indignantly.

Dave was greatly upset. "Why can't I see your father and talk this out?" he asked her.

"That's the thing to do," the girl agreed.

Jeff Smith stayed to guard the flock, while Phil and Dave Horton rode southeast with the cavalcade. Phil pushed his horse close to Lydie's. The sound of her voice stirred him and he paid no attention to the lowering cowboys.

It was dark when they reached the princely B-in-a-Bell which ran thousands of steers. The house was single-storied, of whitened brick, rambling far and wide in the hollow. A large waterhole provided water for stock, for trees and flowers. Fences, barns, smokehouse and springhouse, a big bunkhouse, gave it the look of a small village. Lights blazed, the flickering red of an open fire giving the front main room a cozy appearance.

But a number of cattlemen, fully armed, gathered around the porch, and inside the front room, which buzzed with excitement. Horses stood in the shadows, and the glint of light showed on the metal of rifle barrels and six-guns.

Phil Horton dismounted, stood to help Lydie. The two sheepmen followed the pretty young woman up on the veranda and inside. "Father!" she called. "Here's Mr. David Horton to see you. He's head of the sheepmen."

A growl rose from the ranchers. A peppery voice yelled, "Hell's bells!" A short, wiry man in a blue shirt, black riding pants tucked into expensive halfboots, jumped toward them. He had red hair over a strong face, fiery eyes that showed his commanding nature.

Phil Horton, in his dark-blue suit, curly head bared in the lamplight, calmly faced the unfriendly crowd. Hoofs pounded outside, as horsemen whirled up. A tall, thin man with a grim face heavily bearded, whiskers larded with grey, pushed in.

"Bell," he cried, "the Comanches are pressin' in! I managed to sneak through their lines this morning. And your waterholes have all been poisoned, dead cows everywhere!"

A huge man shoved past him, a man inches over six feet, with a grizzly bear's body. He had a wide, flat nose, flashing eyes, in a horse face, straight black hair showing

17

under the broad fawn Stetson. His high cheek-bones gave him the equine look. Guns, matched Colts trimmed with inlaid mother-of-pearl designs, showed in his sagging holsters.

"Tazewell's right, Bell," he shouted. "I know damn well who laid that pizen too — those consarned sheepmen we chased. They're tryin' to clean the range of cattle and bust us cowmen so's they kin run their lousy sheep in! Yore cows're dyin' by the thousands, there's nuthin' to do but skin 'em and quick, 'fore the buzzards ruin the hides."

Bell's face was purple with suppressed rage. "If yuh're responsible for this, or any of yore danged herders, Horton," he snarled, "Gawd help yuh!"

"What!" yelled Mustang, the man in the fawn Stetson. "This hombre's a sheepman! Lemme at him, curse his stinkin' heart —" He started ferociously toward Dave Horton.

Phil Herren stepped quickly between his father and the furious giant. His clear gaze held Mustang's reddened orbs.

"Outa my way," ordered Mustang, reaching out with a huge paw to sweep Phil from his path, but as his hand touched Phil the sheepman gripped the thick wrist, jerked

18

cleverly, whirling Mustang back against the wall.

With a curse, Mustang recovered, hand flashing to his gun, but Phil Horton, anticipating his move, was in, hard fist smacking against the big man's jaw, rocking him on his heels. As Mustang teetered, he felt the hard cold muzzle of Phil's pistol against his yielding belly.

The scrap had flared and was over in two seconds, but a roar of rage rose from the ranchers.

"Stop — stop." Lydie's voice rang out. Rough and tough as they were, they would listen to a woman, and a pretty one could command them. "Please be quiet," she ordered, "and let Father and Mr. Horton talk this over. There's been a mistake, I'm sure."

"Quiet down, Mustang," Bell snapped. "Wait outside if yuh can't hold yore hosses. Horton, s'pose we go into the side room where we can talk quiet?" He led the way, Dave at his heels, through a hall, turned into a smaller chamber, shut the door.

As Phil stepped back, still watching him closely, the giant swung on his spurs and walked outside, followed by many of the men.

Mustang's horse-face was twisted with

fury, and he gave forth an aura of whiskey.

"You must be hungry," Lydie said to Phil Horton. Her amber eyes shone, and plainly the way he had stood up to Mustang had delighted her. "Come to the kitchen and I'll fix you some food."

He was hungry and he knew she was taking him out of the hostile crowd because she was kind. Through a dining room and a long hall they reached the huge kitchen, with a saddle loft at one side. Lydie brought out food, and they talked together as Phil gratefully ate.

Through an open window, Phil could hear his father's voice and Hell's Bells Bell as they talked. From the corner of his eye he saw a shadowy figure outside, run past the opening. A shot crackled, then a second.

"What was that!" gasped Lydie, jumping up.

Phil Horton threw back his chair, hurried to the window, stuck out his head. Someone in the dark yard fired at him. Lydie seized his shoulder to pull him back. A hoarse cry, "Murder!" came from the room where Bell and Horton were closeted, trying to arrange the trouble on the range.

Phil Horton turned and ran through the hall. The door of the room opened, and Marley Bell leaped out, gun in hand.

"Lamp shot to pieces! Horton's plugged! Gimme a match, Lydie. See how bad it is."

Anguish gripped Phil's heart. He shoved Bell out of the way, leaped into the death room. Lydie struck a match and touched it to a candle wick. The flickering beam rested on the prostrate form crumpled by the open window, blue bullethole through Dave Horton's head from one temple to the other.

"Dead!" Phil gasped.

A grim face stared through the window. It was Jefferson Smith, the old herder.

"C'mon, Phil," he yelled. "Hustle, 'fore they kill yuh too!" Marley Bell, starting back into the room, saw the rising Sharps, leaped away as it blasted its great slug through the door and buried in the wall opposite. Shooting rose outside, and running feet in the hall sent Phil Horton to the window.

"Wait, wait!" Lydie cried.

Shocked and stunned at his father's murder and sure Bell had done it, Horton leaped through the opening. A bunch of men at the front were shooting along the house, and a bullet tore through Phil's jacket, burning his ribs. Jeff Smith grabbed him and they jumped for the shadows. An answering fire at the cowmen, who were led by the giant Mustang, came from close at hand.

"It's Olly Crouse and his herders," Jeff Smith told young Horton. "C'mon, we got hosses."

Sheltered by the stone springhouse at the rear, shooting furious lead at the whooping hombres coming toward them, the half dozen sheepherders mounted and cut off around the waterhole. Olly Crouse, a stout man of fifty, in overalls and a corduroy cap, pushed close to Phil as they rode through the darkness.

"Yore dad's kilt?" he demanded, and when Phil told him, he snarled, "We'll shoot every dirty cowman in the Panhandle! They run my sheep into the river canyon yestiddy and chased me and my boys. Soon after you left, we come on Jeff and your flock; them masked cowmen run your sheep off, and though we killed a few, they beat us off." Jeff and Crouse, with the latter's followers, had headed for the B-in-a-Bell to warn the Hortons.

"We've got to get together," Phil Horton growled. He fought to hold his emotions in check, to think clearly, as he took command which the others granted without question.

"I heard a bunch of sheepmen had gone to Making City," Crouse grunted, as they flew through the night, leaving the ranch behind. "Went to complain to the sheriff 'bout havin' been raided! Huh, fat chance they got! Sheriff was elected by these murderin' cowmen."

Phil Horton thought for a moment. Then he said, "We'll head for Making. If the law won't help us, we can pick up our friends there, at least. C'mon." He turned his horse south.

It was near midnight when they reached Making, the Panhandle metropolis, center for the ranchers for hundreds of miles around, but the town was wide awake, seething with excitement. Saloons ran wide open, and groups of men stood about, discussing the Indian uprising, the ruin of the range and the death of the cattle from poison, or listening to orators. Passing near a large gathering on the Plaza, on their way to the sheriff's office, the little nucleus of sheepmen stopped at a group who was listening to a speaker.

"To hell with Texas!" the man shouted, "what's she ever done for the Panhandle? Austin's too far off to help us. We've got to help ourselves, and quick, or we'll be wiped out. No man is safe!"

The sheriff, "Dog" Wilson, an earnest, heavy looking man with a brown mustache, was just mounting his saddled horse at the jail, in front of which was his office. Phil

Horton pushed up to him.

"Look here, Sheriff Wilson," he said, having asked the official's name when he inquired the way to the jail, "my father, David Horton, was murdered this evening by Marley Bell, at the B-in-a-Bell ranch."

"Huh?" growled Wilson, frowning at the set face of the stalwart young man. "Murdered — by Marley Bell? Say, who're you?"

"My name's Philip Horton. Our sheep and the flocks of my friends have been destroyed by cowmen gangs on this range."

"Sheepmen, huh?" Wilson said gruffly, scowling at Horton. "Some more of yore pals was here, complainin' to me this afternoon. But I ain't got time to ride to the B-in-a-Bell now, even if what yuh say's true, feller. You and yore men have made a lota trouble in the Panhandle and I got my hands full. D'yuh know anything 'bout the pizenin' of the waterholes?

"I'm on my way right now to see 'bout the murder of Charlie Long, a Circle O line-rider they say sheepmen kilt when he caught 'em pizenin' a spring! The whole Panhandle's flared up, what with yuh fellers, and them damn Comanches! I can't handle half the work in this county, and the state ain't sent me no help. If I ketch yuh doin' any shootin', young feller, or find yuh had

24

anything to do with killin' them cattle herds, I'll arrest *you!*"

"Like hell!" snapped Phil. "You won't arrest us. Go bring in Marley Bell for murdering my father!"

"Well, I'll look into that when I get around to it." As Crouse had declared, Sheriff Wilson had been put in office by the powerful Panhandle Grazers. Balked of legal revenge, sure no local jury would convict Marley Bell, Phil Horton led his followers away.

They scouted around and found ten sheepmen, the bunch mentioned by the sheriff, outside a saloon, and, joined by them, rode slowly north along Main Street.

A cavalcade, led by the giant Mustang with whom Horton had clashed at the B-in-a-Bell, swept into town from the north, met them head on. With a hoarse bellow, Mustang opened fire, recognizing Phil Horton.

The sheepmen whirled, backing into the shadows between buildings, drawing their guns in reply. One of young Horton's friends was knocked dead at the first volley; the sheepmen poured back a hot fire that emptied two saddles close to Mustang. Townsmen began to run toward the scene, yelling, joining in.

"Let's ride," Horton ordered, seeing enemies piling up, threatening to surround his small party.

First he must rally the sheepmen, arm them, and then he would fight for his rights. They faded away into the darkness.

Over the great Panhandle hovered death. In towns to the south and west, rioting crowds howled at the words of orators who cursed Texas, demanding secession on the grounds that since Texas failed to protect them and maintain order, they must form their own commonwealth and with their tax income and state organization restore peace to the Panhandle!

CHAPTER II
SAVE TEXAS!

"Hurry!" Cap'n Bill McDowell's voice was harsh with a stridency almost panic.

No one who knew McDowell would believe it was a personal fear; he was too brave for that. In his riding days he had charged Indians and gunmen armies single-handed. The old Frontier-model Colts on his desk had brought honor and peace to Texas.

It was for Texas that he feared, as he looked up into the strong face of the tall man.

"The trouble's spread like wildfire, Hatfield. Ev'ry hour counts. Maybe too late now!"

Jim Hatfield, known as the Lone Wolf because he chose to ride alone on dangerous missions, held the burning eyes of his captain. Hatfield's grey-green orbs, shaded by black lashes, were icy as an Arctic sea. Inches over six feet, powerful shoulders to match, he listened to his orders.

There was a majestic calm about the famous Ranger. The deep chest rose and fell, no break in the steady rhythm of the never-quavering heart. Single-handed, with his deadly Colts, Hatfield had defeated the most vicious killers and their murderous bands.

Jim Hatfield's reputation for dealing with such, who plotted against the Lone Star State, made evil men curse the day he was born. Many had died so cursing him while others, hot-eyed and broken, eked out their miserable days behind prison steel.

The muscles of Hatfield's long arms were like supple metal cords; the slim hands, at ease now, could in action flash with the speed of a sunbeam. His strength matched his great frame, and was magnified by clever tricks of training, by the cool, keen brain in the handsome, black-haired head. Bronzed by the biting wind of the norther, by the blazing desert sun, the Ranger's rugged face was lean, not an ounce of superfluous flesh was upon him. A broad mouth relieved the stern lines of his countenance.

His voice was soft, drawling, yet it held a timbre which forced men to listen. "Yuh callate it's more than a local sheep-cattle war?"

McDowell's gnarled fist made the ink-well jump. "Yes, Jim. This trouble's deep and

28

tall. I got reports from a dozen county sheriffs, sayin' invadin' sheepmen pizened the waterholes and shot down cowboys to clear the range of cattle. The Comanches are on the warpath in the west." He lowered his voice, vibrant with excitement: "Here's what worries the Guvnor most — me, too! It's civil war in the Panhandle and North-west.

"Federal intervention's jest eased off Texas, so we got to handle this ourselves and pronto, 'fore they send back Federal officials to take charge. Texas is in real danger, Jim. Our state we've fit so hard to make the best place on earth for decent folks may be split! They're sayin' in the Panhandle that Texas is too big and unwieldy and they want to form their own commonwealth. Claim Austin's too far off to maintain order, and it seems so, with this war and the Indians roused agin."

The coiled-spring muscles of the great fighting man lay in somnolent poise, his whole body having the grace of a leashed tiger. He stared past McDowell's silvered head.

"Texas!" he growled.

McDowell, too, felt that fierce loyalty for his state. Too old to ride on such a mission he could but pick his men. Looking at Jim

Hatfield he knew he had chosen well; no one else could deal with such a far-reaching, dynamite-charged situation, Hatfield's fighting power being matched by an Empire builder's vision.

"We'll be ridin'," said the Lone Wolf simply. By "we" he meant himself and the golden sorrel who champed outside.

McDowell accompanied him to the door, touched his gun arm. "Good luck to that. Yuh'll need it, Jim!"

Hatfield's leather faintly creaked, silver spurs tinkling as he moved. "Making City's capital of the Panhandle country, and that's where the wust of this sheep-cattle war has hit. Yuh'll find Virgil Tazewell, an old-time trapper, a man to ride the river with. Virg and me trapped the Rockies together. He's got a hide warehouse and tradin' post there in Making.

"I'll call in as many Rangers as I kin and have 'em report to yuh in Making. But we may be too late, so hurry!" He trailed Hatfield out into the sunshine.

The Lone Wolf patted Goldy; the sorrel, sleek with the best of care bucked as the lithe rider settled in the high-pronged saddle. Warsack fastened at the cantle, rifle snugged in leather sling under left leg, Hatfield swung Goldy, pointed northwest. With a wave of his long hand to McDowell he cantered toward a land of death, of evil forces so potent they threatened to engulf the mighty commonwealth.

Austin soon was behind, the golden sorrel's gait easy but pace-eating. Goldy was a fit mount for the untiring Ranger, who could go days on sleep snatches, on swallows of alkali water, tightening his belt a notch for a meal.

"Split Texas!" the man growled, and Goldy laid back his velvet ears, snorted in disdain.

Ever upward rose the trail. Across rivers dangerous with quicksands, through grazing lands and into the mountains moved the man on the golden horse.

Following the Salt Fork of the Brazos, he came to the great plains, four thousand feet above sea-level.

Hatfield noted the increasing scarcity of range cattle, usually so numerous here, and the number of bleaching steer skulls and bowed rib-bones was appalling. Buzzards dotted the sky and the mesquite was alive with coyotes and other scavengers.

He was not many miles from Making City, the Panhandle Metropolis, when he ran into trouble. The Lone Wolf's gray-green eyes seldom were still but moved from point to point with the eternal vigilance of the wilderness man. Goldy might be counted on to warn of danger so Hatfield did not overlook the sorrel's uneasy twitch; though the horizon seemed innocent, Hatfield was aware something was about to occur.

And a rider popped up from nowhere — the Ranger knew he had been sitting his horse, motionless, blending with a mesquite patch and the gray rocks.

"Howdy," the hombre sang out. He had a very broad, squat body, husky all the way through, clad in chaps and vest over a maroon shift. His face was bronzed and pleasant enough, only the creases about his eyes, that gave him a foxy look, might have warned an alert observer that he was sharper than he appeared. His slate-colored Stetson was trimmed with a three-inch wide band made from a dried rattlesnake's skin; a vermilion circle decorated it in front.

Hatfield nodded as he faced the husky man. The latter grinned and asked, "Have a smoke?" and held out a sack of tobacco and packet of papers.

"Thanks, but I jest throwed one away."

"Headin' for Making? I'll ride along with yuh."

Hatfield, aware of the fellow's swift, appraising scrutiny, shrugged and they went on together. "I ride for the Circle 2," the hombre chatted, "but most of our stock was pizened by them dirty sheepherders. There's a war on and strangers ain't welcome."

"Yuh mean me?"

"No, no, I ain't that sort," disclaimed the rider as though shocked at the suggestion. "But mebbe I kin help yuh if yuh're huntin' someone perticular."

Trying to pump the tall jigger was discouraging. The husky man's horse shouldered the sorrel and Goldy shied to the right and snorted. They had trotted but a hundred yards when again Goldy was bumped, edged a few feet farther north.

"Now what's he after?" mused Hatfield; he had refused the makings, for it is too easy for the donor to reach over and seize a gun-wrist while the victim's hands are occupied with a smoke.

Hatfield waited for the next collision and it came soon, the husky man swearing and cruelly bitting his horse as though punishing him for unruliness. The road looked clear but, topping a slight rise, Hatfield observed a patch of weathered rocks thick with cactus growth and mesquite. He decided the husky man was shoving him to it. The Lone Wolf touched Goldy with his right knee and the powerful sorrel made a sudden swing left, knocking the other horse aside. "Sorry," Hatfield drawled.

The hombre gave him a sharp glance. "Now look," he growled, voice no longer soft, "I tell yuh this is dangerous country."

"But it's still free, ain't it?" By a spur touch Hatfield completed his maneuver so his companion was between him and the rocks.

Three men, bandannas drawn up to gleaming, hard eyes, bobbed up from the cover. They toted sawed-off shotguns and, making the best of a bad job, spoiled by the Ranger's quick action, they threw down on the riders.

"Hey, we want yore money and hosses. Get off and deliver or we'll blow yuh to hell!" the leader ordered.

"Holdup," gasped the cowboy. "We better let 'em have our stuff, mister —"

"Stay right where yuh are," Hatfield said softly. The husky man glanced back, saw the Ranger's steady Colt trained on his spine; panic flared in his eyes and he remained nailed as he was. If the trio pulled triggers they would hit him first.

The three masked hombres started at them. "Put up that gun 'fore yuh get hurt," the leader bawled, catching the glint of sun on Hatfield's weapon. He fired a warning load from his shotgun that whooshed over the heads of the mounted pair.

Goldy stood firm, trained to such work, but the husky man's horse, either through fright or her rider's wish, began to dance, half-exposing the Ranger. The masked leader was bringing his snub-nosed shotgun to cover Hatfield, and the Ranger fired, his slug smashing the gunman's thigh. As the leader hit the dirt, Hatfield whirled Goldy, felt the wind of a hastily fired, bunched shot.

The officer's calloused thumb rose, a second masked bandit dropped his shotgun, doubled up out of the fight. In these second-fractions the Lone Wolf's grim face had not changed. There was no apparent hurry, for a trained gun-fighter takes his time within limits, for accuracy. The third of the masked hombres, appalled at the slaughter of his mates, dropped his gun and jumped frantically for the rocks.

Hatfield, Colt steady, met the gaze of the husky man who had tried to push him into the trap. The pale orbs were bulging and the husky hombre seemed to find difficulty in swallowing.

"Why — that was good shootin'," he gasped hoarsely.

"Unbuckle yore gunbelt and get down."

"Why, what's wrong?"

35

"Drop yore guns!"

Unable to meet the Lone Wolf's steady eyes, the husky man obeyed. He cursed but none too boldly and at Hatfield's command walked toward the rocks. The Ranger kicked the other horse and sent it running off. To the south dust rose. To the north, more riders were approaching. Hatfield cantered off at an angle, heading again for Making.

The encounter told him the approaches to the troubled country were picketed; those coming in had heard the shooting and were hurrying to join the sentries. His experienced eye had told him that the supposed bandits were not cowmen or sheepmen; they looked to him like gun-fighters and their actions were professional. With a burst of speed the golden sorrel carried him over the next wave of the prairie ocean, on toward Making, hub of the Panhandle.

The city sprawled on gray flats, buildings visible at a distance across the level reaches. The Ranger rode in from the southeast, crossed a railroad spur, looking over the town.

Main Street was wide, packed by the passage of many hoofs and wagon-wheels, lined with buildings of sheet-iron and imported timber, rutted side lanes branching off here and there. Gaily colored signs announced the purpose of the various stores and saloons; along the track were two large buildings and over one was a red sign reading:

VIRGIL TAZEWELL. HIDES AND PELTS.

Though the day was fair, the central plaza and the streets were deserted. Hatfield dismounted at the road side of Tazewell's warehouse, hitched up his gun-belt, shook dust from his clothes, and as he ducked under the hitchrail he heard from the north end the sound of cheering.

The door was open, and he stepped into a small office which reeked of acrid odors, hides and tanning chemicals. A man snored in a chair, booted feet on the desk. Hatfield shook him till he opened his eyes.

"Tazewell here?" the Ranger demanded.

"Oh — nope, he's at the meetin'. Ev'rybuddy is."

A photograph hung over the table, of a lean man with a partially bald head and a sharp nose. "That Tazewell?"

"Yeah, that's him." The fellow at the desk, fully awake now, watched him. "What yuh want with him?"

"I'll tell him that myself." Hatfield nodded, remounted and rode north, past the wide plaza with its brick jail, and reached the end of the houses. He left Goldy and strolled toward the large crowd of people listening to an orator who stood on a platform in the center. Several hundred citizens were present, densely packed together, and the tall officer could not immediately locate Virgil Tazewell.

The speaker's commanding, fiery voice drove his words forcibly to Hatfield's attention: "We must have peace! The violent men who disturb our daily pursuits shall be curbed. These cowardly gunmen have no right to endanger our children and ourselves in their private feuds! Their bullets fly in our towns and through the open range. The Panhandle must be made safe for decent citizens. This sheep-cattle war is an abomination, a few selfish, greedy men ruin our land, fight each other while the redskins strike our western border —"

The orator was a short but not unimpressive figure. His head was large and well-shaped, bared to the sun. A shock of thick black hair curved on his noble white brow, over a determined face with flashing black eyes. He gesticulated with well-kept white hands as he spoke. A thin hombre in chaps, spurred black boots, vest over a red shirt, wide Stetson, six-guns hanging in studded cartridge belt, interrupted the speaker with a harsh shout:

"I'll kill ev'ry sheepman I see! Dang their dirty hides, they ruint me, Farnsworth. This is cow country, savvy?"

Hoots drowned him out. "Shut up, Mike Gans!" "Boo!"

Hatfield stared at Gans. The man had a cast in one eye and a thin face, fringed by stringy brown hair. Gans' face was twisted with rage.

Farnsworth, the orator, raised a hand to still the mob. Hundreds of animated faces showed in the throng, cowboys, tradesmen, farmers; townsmen, and black-frocked, solemn-visaged gamblers. Farnsworth resumed his speech:

"I tell you the cattlemen and sheepherders have caused this trouble. These feudal ranchers who claim vast stretches with no legal title other than the law accords every homesteader! Their guns keep thousands from their birthright, from these plains which will blossom as the rose. They will finally bring on our heads the power of the Federal government which cannot ignore this civil war — yes, this is war.

"Do you want Federal intervention again, the self-seeking tyranny of venal men?" asked the speaker. "Our taxes are paid to

Texas. Surely we are entitled to protection, but if it does not come we must act ourselves —"

A pistol cracked on the taut air. The bullet sang like an angry hornet, the stocky speaker staggered and gripped the rail with both white hands, a widening, red stain on his broad cheek.

"I'll teach yuh to talk so 'bout cattlemen!" an angry voice howled.

Chapter III
Mustang

Farnsworth after his first involuntary twitch, did not quail. He stood proudly erect, defying them all.

"Murder me if you dare!" he shouted.

Hatfield was already in action, moving toward the hombre who had tried to drygulch the speaker. The Ranger could make out the fresh gash in the platform rail where the slug had hit, evidently sending a jagged splinter into Farnsworth's face. The mob began to mill, and the yells swelled to a mighty roar.

The assassin wore a cowboy outfit, chaps and vest, wide hat; he had a dark, savage face which Hatfield glimpsed as the gunman leaped a fence where a saddled horse waited.

"I defy you," Farnsworth yelled, shaking his fist. "I defy Marley Bell and his paid killers. I defy the men whose only law is murder!"

Moving with a panther's grace to stop the savage, dark-faced gunman, Hatfield violently collided with a huge man. By accident or design a sharp elbow was driven into his stomach, the unexpected impact knocking the Ranger off balance. He caught himself quickly, thinking the bump accidental, for the people were all shifting. Howls of rage came from the throats of the crowd. Hatfield found, as he tried to step around the big hombre, that again he was blocked, since the fellow had jumped to cut him off from the fleeing gunman, stopped his play.

"What's yore idea, runnin' into me like that, stranger?" the giant snarled.

The savage, black-haired gunman was across the short space and behind the houses; a defiant cowboy whoop came back on the breeze. Thanks to the huge hombre, Hatfield had lost the opportunity of stopping the killer. With a touch of impatience that did not show in the set lines of his stern face, he swung on the man who had spoiled his game.

It was literally eye-to-eye, for the other was as tall as Hatfield, heavier through the hips, where the sun glinted on six-shooters trimmed with a complicated mother-of-pearl design. Into huge halfboots, turned over at the spurred heels by the bow of an inveterate rider's legs, were tucked tight-fitting riding pants.

The man's hands were like raw hams, flecked with black hairs, hanging at the end of apishly curved mighty arms attached to wide shoulders. His brow was creased in fury, and the deepset eyes, over high-cheek bones, gave him a horsy look. Over the sullen mouth was a squashed nose. His whole appearance was untamed, fierce, brutally self-assured.

"Yuh're in my road," Hatfield drawled.

"Yore road to where?" The giant pined for a scrap.

The Ranger's hands hung easily at his slim hips; he watched his opponent's gun hand.

"Hey, Mustang!" Gans, the wild-eyed rancher who had interrupted Farnsworth, shoved through the crowd.

Mustang's play, saving that gunman, was only a straw showing which way the wind blew — yet, if this aptly named Mustang forced a fight, Hatfield was ready. From broad experience in such affrays he knew it had come to that. Like filings attracted to a suddenly charged magnet, sharp-eyed hombres with ready Colts hurried toward the two big fellows. There flashed over the Ranger the surety that Mustang had planted them all, knew of the attempt to kill Farnsworth, and the covering of the gunman.

Only a moment had passed. Lightning-swift, the thoughts raced through the Lone Wolf's brain, cool as his fighting heart which never speeded its beat, allowing perfect coordination and timing between that brain and the trained muscles of his body.

"Wait'll I take keer of this skunk, Mike!" Mustang snapped, his great paw starting for his gun.

Hatfield's Colt slashed out, the sharp sight cutting across Mustang's ferocious face, stabbing him back. Mustang's slug hit the dirt between the Ranger's spread boots.

But the mob was moving, welling after the fleeing gunman, and shouting men shoved between Hatfield and Mustang. A hand grasped at the Ranger's throat as one of Mustang's friends reached for him; he swung to drive his fist in a swift punch that jolted the man's head back, glazed his eyes.

Then Hatfield was forcibly pushed away from his opponent, deafened by the roar of the crowd. As a powerful stream splits two floating objects, Hatfield and Mustang were separated. The Ranger was carried along in the crush toward Main Street.

The attempted assassination broke up the meeting. The rider had escaped, was only a dust cloud on the plain heading west. Hatfield shoved out of the hurrying throng, paused between two houses. An eye peeled for Mustang, he went back to pick up Goldy. Mounting, he started the sorrel along a narrow lane which ran parallel with Main Street, back toward Tazewell's.

An hombre in cowboy clothes, whom Hatfield spotted as one of those who had tried to lay hands on him during his brush with Mustang, suddenly jumped out from behind a barn. Goldy shied, forehoofs leaving the dirt; the armed man hurriedly fired, and Hatfield felt the sear of the bullet along his thigh as it cut his chaps, missing because of Goldy's quick movement.

The fellow's small eyes glittered as he again took aim. Hatfield's six-shooter flashed with terrific speed of which he was capable. The Ranger's slug hit the gunman in the shoulder, knocked him down. More men ran from the street, and Hatfield touched Goldy with a spur, darting past the opening, hearing the lead whirl behind him. He swung through to Main, and reaching Tazewell's, left Goldy in a shed at the rear and entered the office.

A tall, lean man stood, looking at him as Hatfield came in. The Ranger glanced curiously at the famous scout and trapper.

The slender figure was clad in buckskin,

pants fringed by uneven strips, mocassins on long, straight feet. A clipped yellow beard, streaked with white, was shaped to the pointed chin, the nose curving like an eagle's beak. Myriad seams showed around the deep-set light-blue eyes which fixed Hatfield with the penetration of sharp knife points.

Every facet, every feature of the man indicated a keenness of perception rivaling that of the Lone Wolf. The lean man had taken off his coonskin hat, held it in one bony hand; his hair was straw-colored, and like his beard, larded with the hoar of age. The portrait on the wall was only a colorless shadow of the hombre facing Jim Hatfield.

"Tazewell?" drawled Hatfield. The assistant was gone and they stood together in the office.

The lean man nodded, the famous scout running an appraising glance over the powerful fighting machine that was the Ranger. He spoke, voice soft and slow, but with a timbre that demanded attention. "What kin I do for you?"

Hatfield opened his slim, strong hand, and the light from the door fell upon the silver star set on a silver circle, emblem of the Texas Rangers. "Cap'n McDowell sent me.

I'm Jim Hatfield."

The eyes shot forth a sudden flash, and the buckskin swished as Tazewell shifted. Then he held out his hand. "You needn't add any more. I've heard of you." After a pause, he ordered, "Come in back. If there's anything I can do, I want you to tell me."

The trapper led the way, moving with a wild animal's grace. The warehouse was filled with cattlehides ready to ship. Pelts were here, too, beaver and bear, wolf and over all the musty odor. Tazewell swung left, entered a little den where stood a rough bunk, a cookstove, guns and traps and clothes spread about.

Hatfield wished to make his arrangements quickly. Tazewell shoved over a whiskey bottle, squatted on his heels.

"McDowell," the Ranger explained, "callated yuh could give me an idee as to how things stand in the Panhandle. I'm here to stop the trouble."

The lean trapper stared sombrely at the rough brown boards of the wall. He cleared his throat, asked, "You're alone?"

Hatfield nodded. "Scoutin' the way."

"I see." He added, "Cards on the table?"

"From ace to deuce."

"Things 're bad. The Comanches have raided the western border, angry because settlers have invaded their huntin' grounds. You've heard of the sheep-cattle war that's swept the range, a dozen men have died, many more wounded. Trade's stopped, save for hides from thousands of cows pizened by the sheepmen."

"Yuh're shore the sheepmen laid the stuff?"

"Who else? They did it in revenge at bein' chased off. And once they clear the range they can bring in their sheep, those flocks that the cattlemen haven't destroyed."

"I note yuh got plenty of them cowhides."

Tazewell shook his head gloomily. "I was away on a huntin' trip, across the Staked Plain, and I got back too late. Other dealers beat me to it. Those I have were bought before the market broke, since the cowmen could only dump their hides. I have contracts, signed before the break, to fill. I lose my shirt, since the price now is small. The sheepmen ruint me, too."

"Who got most of the hides, then?"

Tazewell hesitated, then shrugged. "You see the big warehouse down the track? That belongs to Frank Ulman. He's bought in thousands for a song. The sheepmen sifted over the hull northwest range sprinkling pizen —" He broke off, stiffening, a startled gleam in his keen eyes as Hatfield, with a

48

panther's lithe speed, glided to him, put a hand to the man's lips.

"Mighty dry weather." the Ranger said loudly. In Tazewell's ear he quickly whispered, "Someone sneakin' up on us — say I'm yore new pardner. I want to stay covered."

Tazewell relaxed, nodded. The Lone Wolf went to the door, stood at one side, reached out and opened it. Mustang, the big fellow, and a dozen men were tiptoeing across the warehouse floor, trying to reach the side room. Hatfield's keen senses had caught the creak of a loose board.

"Why, howdy, Flowers," cried Tazewell. "What kin I do for you?"

Mustang Flowers paused, feet widespread. His heavy jaw dropped as he lowered at Hatfield. "Say," he snarled, "yuh jest shot a pal of mine!" His face burned brick-red under his tan and a smear of clotted blood showed where Hatfield had raked him with his gun barrel.

"Wait," Tazewell snapped. "This man's the son of an old trail-mate of mine, Mustang. Meet Jim Harrison, my new pardner. If he shot anyone, that hombre asked for it!"

Tazewell was quick of wit, and he was looked up to as a personage, even Mustang Flowers backed down.

"He's all-fired brash with his guns," Mustang growled.

The Ranger coolly eyed the gang. They wore cowboy accoutrements, riding boots and pants, vests over flannel shirts, high hats — Hatfield suddenly realized something. Though the hats were of different shapes and colors, every one save Mustang's was trimmed with a rattlesnake skin band, a vermilion circle splashed in front!

The husky man he had encountered had worn such a decoration, and, come to think of it, so had the fellows who seemed Mustang's pals at the meeting. Why? the Ranger asked himself. It would be to mark friend to friend, of course, and that denoted a large organization, so large that all its members would not know each other save by this uniform marking.

"Sorry 'bout yore pard, Flowers," Hatfield said. "He scairt my horse, jumpin' out so sudden and shootin' at me. I figgered he was drunk and jest winged him."

Mustang had lost his decisiveness; suspicion glowed in his red-rimmed eyes as he glanced at Trapper Tazewell, whose ready explanation was designed to allay distrust of the Ranger.

"We'll head across the Staked Plain," prattled on Tazewell, feigning to be unaware of the taut air, "and set our traps in the mountains."

"Huh." Flowers stared at Hatfield. Whether he feared the slim hands would move too fast for him or whether it was Tazewell's okay, he said, "Well, be keerful how yuh yank yore hawgleg after this."

"Meet you over at the Steer's Head in ten minutes, Mustang," Tazewell said. "Drinks 're on me."

Flowers nodded, swung and stalked off.

"Who is he?" inquired Hatfield.

"Oh, a cowman of sorts, he's got a bunch of friends, though he's new to the Panhandle. Tough, ain't he?"

Hatfield shrugged. "I'd like to see some of those hides, off the poisoned cows."

Tazewell led him to the rear yard, where cowhides were drying on long stands. Carefully he looked them over.

"What've you found?" asked Tazewell curiously as he saw Hatfield's frown, the Ranger rubbing his fingers across the inner surface of a stretched skin. He held out his hand, palm up.

Tazewell stared at the white grains sticking to Hatfield's finger-tips. "White arsenic!" Hatfield exclaimed. "Works into the hide."

Tazewell was startled. "Sheepmen carry

pizen for varmints, don't they?"

"Not this stuff, it's usually strychnine. Yuh must know that, in yore trappin' work."

"Sure, sure. It surprised me at first. You're all-fired smart, Jim. Now suppose we go and play Mustang Flowers along a bit at the saloon?"

Hatfield followed him to the sidewalk. Making was an important place, and they swung quickly beneath the continuous wooden awnings to the Steer's Head, a popular drinking-place filled with cowboys, gamblers, townsmen. Dusk was at hand and the oil lamps had been lighted.

As they entered the wide front door, Tazewell nudged the Ranger. "That yellow-faced hombre is Frank Ulman, the dealer who got most of them hides, Jim!"

Here was a man who must be making money out of the Panhandle's calamity. The Ranger looked Ulman over. Ulman wore a well-tailored black suit, a conservative black Stetson on his narrow head, covered by close-clipped curly black hair. His complexion was unhealthily sallow; he had a small bristly mustache and clenched in buck teeth was a long cigar, eyes narrowed in the ring smoke.

His frock coat was unbuttoned, disclosing a purple silk vest across which hung a solid-gold chain. Tazewell paused and slapped him on the shoulder, saying jovially, "Meet my new assistant, Jim Harrison, Frank." Everybody knew the old trapper, he was very popular.

Ulman's veiled gaze met Hatfield's; he nodded shortly. "Drop round some day when I ain't busy, young feller!"

"Hey, Tazewell!" That was Mustang Flowers, shouting at them from the far end of the huge room.

Tazewell approached Mustang Flowers. Hatfield followed, taking in the crowd. Now he was hunting for it he noted many of the rattlesnake hatbands; while not an uncommon trimming, the vermilion circle cinched it. The distinctive mark pointed to a large organization.

As they stood at the bar a commotion sounded up front and a compact body of men swept in. At their head was a short, wiry hombre, fifty-dollar boots on his small feet; he had red hair breaking out under his fawn Stetson, a strong, sharp-cut face, with flashing eyes indicating an imperious nature. Guns rode at his waist, and those following him were heavily armed save for one person held inside the bunch. The man who stood out was a stout fellow of fifty, hair gray at the temples; he wore plain shoes and blue overalls. It was Olly Crouse, Phil Horton's sheepman follower.

The cowmen stalked to the bar. "Hey, there's Marley Bell and his riders," Flowers cried. "They've snaffled a sheepman."

"Hold it," ordered Tazewell. "See what they do."

Bell threw money on the bar. "Drinks," he shouted. "Step up — you, too, sheepman. Wet yore whistle. Last chance."

Citizens edged away. Too many bullets had been flying around to take chances. Marley Bell, after draining his glass in one swallow, swung and swept the room with his eyes, looking for enemies. He saw one, for he hitched up his gun-belt and swaggered like a fighting cock across the place, weaving among the tables.

Bell set himself before a round table at which sat John Farnsworth, the orator. Farnsworth had a bandage on his cheek and frowned at Bell as the cattle king, arms akimbo, stood sneering at him.

"Hell's bells, Farnsworth," the cowman bawled in a loud voice, "I hear yuh made a speech against me this afternoon! Fair warnin' — if yuh don't shut yore trap I'll do it for yuh. This is cow country and it's stayin' so!"

Farnsworth shoved back his chair, saying,

"I'm not armed, Bell. I'm not your sort. I
—"

Hatfield, watching the play, suddenly grew
aware of a man who had burst into the
saloon. It was one of the husky hombres of
the hard eyes who had tried to waylay him
on his way in.

CHAPTER IV
LYNCH LAW

The husky man saw Hatfield an instant later, since he was heading straight toward him. He stopped, uttered a whoop of alarm. "Hey, Mustang! That big jigger there shot Jake and Arizony!"

Flowers jumped, turned as the Ranger cleared his throat. "Who, him?" A thick thumb indicated Hatfield.

"Mustang," drawled the Lone Wolf, "if they were pals of yores, don't blame me. I figgered it was a holdup. They said so."

"He's lyin'! He opened up on us without warnin'," the excited hombre yelled.

Hatfield was watching Mustang for the horseman's decision; he knew what it was the instant Flowers made it. Tazewell stood, frozen, as Flowers, with the speed of legerdemain flashed a huge paw toward his pearl-trimmed Colt. Then Mustang's hand paused, slowly and gingerly left the vicinity of his gun; the Colt made a soft sound as it

56

dropped back into its holster. The gunman was staring into the round black muzzle of Jim Hatfield's pistol.

A fraction of a second later the Ranger's gun spat but not into Mustang. Hatfield had shifted, seeing the husky hombre, thinking himself hidden by Mustang's broad figure, go for his hogleg. A bullet tore low along the floor, plugged into the bar; Hatfield's had caught the husky man in the thigh, and the breaking bone made a horrid crunch. The husky man fell heavily, fainting in the pain, all fight gone out of him for a long time.

Acrid powder smoke slowly rose to the hanging lamps. Silence fell upon the saloon, a startled silence that was so thick it could have been cut with a knife.

Mustang Flowers broke it. He croaked, "Awright, mister. You win." He looked at his glass, raised it slowly, both hands in plain sight. Gulping down a drink, Mustang wiped his lips with the back of his hand. "Yuh're fast, Harrison."

No one else seemed to wish to try a shot at the tall jigger. Aware of hostile eyes, as he made a practiced survey Hatfield saw a tiny, ugly man with a patch on his eye. His neck was stuck out, and his good orb was balefully fixed upon the Ranger. He had one hand stuck into the pocket of his greasy gray suit coat, but as he found Hatfield watching him he sat back in his chair. Men looked away from the tall Ranger's cold gray-green gaze, feigned to be busy with their own pursuits. Marley Bell, who had watched the play, came slowly back to his friends.

"C'mon," the cattlemen's chief ordered. "Bring that sheepman, boys. We got to hustle."

Their grim, determined faces told Hatfield what they were contemplating. Hatfield, feeling the tense air, wanted to see what he might do about the situation. It would be simply another brand cast on the blazing fire of horror that burned the Panhandle. Two primary tasks faced him: he must arrange a truce between the sheepmen and cattlemen, and pacify the Comanches.

But in the back of his keen brain he was turning over what he had observed. Besides Marley Bell and his crew, and the opposing sheepmen, there was Mustang Flowers, who appeared to hold sway over an even greater number of gun-fighters. Mustang was maintaining a picket line around Making. Only one of Marley Bell's boys wore a rattlesnake hatband and that had not the vermilion circle on it.

"Figger I'll be ridin'," drawled Hatfield. "Thanks for the drinks."

Flowers grunted. He did not look up from his glass as Hatfield, trailed by the lean Tazewell, started out. Bell was leaving, his men shoving Olly Crouse before them. No one made any move to stop them.

"You sure make things hum," Tazewell exploded, as they hit the sidewalk. "Never saw anyone beat Flowers to the draw!"

Bell and his men were mounted, heading north. The Ranger, with long strides, reached Goldy and swung a long leg across his saddle.

"Where you bound?" the trapper inquired.

Hatfield jerked a thumb after the cattlemen. "I mean to stop that."

Tazewell's narrowed eyes gleamed in admiration. "Alone, eh? I b'lieve you'll try! I'm goin' along." He mounted and rode beside Hatfield, out of Making, along a beaten track that wound across the moonlit prairie, patched with black mesquite shadows. As they cantered in Bell's dust, Hatfield asked,

"Yuh heard this talk of splittin' Texas?"

The trapper drew in a deep breath. "I have. They say Austin's too fur off and doesn't give a hoot in hell what happens to us so long as we pay our taxes. Panhandle citizens want to form a new state, from the Pecos to the Red, Longitude 100. We could use our taxes to pay for our own protection, form our own Rangers — not that I agree, mind you."

"Me either," growled the Ranger.

A mile out of Making, the city's glow red in the sky, Bell's party swung off the trail along the lip of a deep arroyo. Jim Hatfield saw ahead the sombre outline of a lone tree, black against the yellow moon. It was high enough to hang a man from.

As Hatfield and Tazewell approached, they were challenged by a Bell rider. "What's up?" Tazewell inquired.

"Oh, hello, Virg," Marley Bell called. "If yuh wanta watch, get down and do so. Who's that with yuh?"

"Jim Harrison, my new pardner."

At Bell's order dried brush was hastily collected and set afire. In the ruby light Marley Bell came over and looked up into Hatfield's set face.

"Oh, yuh're the jigger who called Mustang, huh? That was mighty quick play, mister."

The horses stood in a group, reins dragging, as the dismounted cowmen gathered around Olly Crouse. The stout sheepman was gulping and his face worked nervously, but he did not whine. A lariat was shaken out, and one end tossed over the tree limb, the noose held by a Bell man, ready to cast over Crouse's head. A horse was led over to do the jerking.

"Got anything to say?" Bell demanded.

"No," growled Crouse, "except to go to hell!"

"I'll see yuh later when I git there," Bell snapped. "Want a cigarette?" He passed Crouse the makings.

All the cowboys were watching their enemy, the crackling brush fire cast dancing shadows over the scene. As the Ranger, determined to prevent the lynching, took a step forward, he felt a tremendous breath pass his cheek. A furious, deadly "whoosh," then a thunderous explosion booming across the flats, told the large caliber of the gun. The Stetson on Marley Bell's red head flew off, strap snapped, hit the ground, ripped to pieces. Bell staggered, half turning around, face dazed; his hand flew to his head and it came away, smeared with blood.

On the echoes of the explosion crashed a volley, flashes from about them, and the horse by the tree shrieked, tumbled in a heap. One of Bell's cowboys whirled and fell flat on his face. Another cursed as his arm went limp. Then the rest had whipped out their guns, jumping away from the light.

Olly Crouse moved with surprising speed, seizing the first instants of confusion to make his escape. He dove past one of his startled captors, knocking him over with his lowered head, and bounded into the bushes. Bell and his cowboys began shooting furiously into the outlying shadows, bullets ripping through the mesquite, plugging dust up from the dirt.

"This way, Olly!" a voice shouted.

The pounding hoofs of retreating horses rang in the smoky air, with the booming guns and whoops of fighting men. "Get to your ponies," screeched Marley Bell. "There's on'y a few of 'em. Hustle!"

But bullets from the bushes had thrown the band of mustangs into a maddened snarl. Riders fought their horses, trying to untangle them. Finally a few mounted, Bell among them, and started in pursuit after the shadowy figures of retreating sheepmen who had attacked to save their friend Crouse. Already they were well out and away, headed west.

Hatfield whistled and Goldy trotted obediently up to him. He mounted and followed along with the infuriated cowmen. On the level space, broken by rocks and mesquite clumps, he could see the hazes of dust rising as the sheepmen split, riding hell-for-leather from their enemies, who outnumbered them.

A sudden whoop of triumph from Bell's lips sent Hatfield galloping that way. One of the sheepman had gone down, as his horse's hoof broke through a gopher hole, tossing the rider headlong to the ground. He rolled over and over, gained his feet, emptying a revolver back at his pursuers as he started to run. Hot bullets beat about him as the cowmen whirled from both sides, and a lariat whizzed out. The fighting sheepman was yanked off his feet, and dragged back along the plain.

"Bring him to the fire," ordered Marley Bell.

The prisoner was pulled, like a roped steer, over the rough earth. Marley Bell dismounted, snapped, "Some of yuh boys watch out, so's they can't rush us again." More brush was tossed on the ruby embers and the fire rose high.

"Hell's bell's!" roared Marley, as he stared at the prisoner. "It's Phil Horton!"

Horton stood, chin up, defying his enemies. His blue clothes were ripped, crusted with dirt, and his right cheek, which had dragged the plain, was bleeding and stained. His powerful chest spasmodically rose and fell, for he was winded from his run.

Since his father's death Phil Horton had lost pounds off his sturdy frame; the hit-and-run existence made him look gaunt.

Horton had managed to collect forty sheepmen and expected more from Oklahoma as he had sent messengers to fetch them. He was a hard looking customer, muscles like steel bands, red fury in his heart against Marley Bell and the cattlemen who had killed his father and ruined him and his friends.

"So we got yuh," snarled Bell. The chief's hot eyes drilled the young man. Hatred welled in Horton's breast and his lip curled contemptuously off his even white teeth. He laughed in Bell's furious face.

"Yuh've pulled some skunk tricks on my range," rasped on Marley. "Outside of ruin-in' us by pizenin' our cows yuh've plugged half a dozen of my friends. And why? For no reason at all, jest 'cause yuh're a thievin', murderin' devil!"

Horton laughed harshly. "No reason?" he growled. "Who shot my father? Who drove our sheep over the cliffs?"

"Not me," Bell declared.

"Some of yore men, at yore order. What's the diff?"

"We didn't start this war. None of us kilt

64

yore dad."

"You're a sorrel-topped liar," Horton said coldly.

"Aw, let's get it over with," an impatient cowboy snarled. "Here's the rope, boss."

They pressed in on Phil, but Bell raised an imperious hand.

"Let him have his say," the rancher ordered. Marley was conducting a rough court of justice, according to his lights. These men were fiercely individualistic; when they considered it necessary they acted as law officers, judges and executioners in a wild, rough land.

Horton knew that. He had something to say and he began to enumerate the crimes of the cattlemen, but hardly had he begun when hoofs pounded from the direction of Making. A large gang of riders, wearing snakebands around their hats and led by a gigantic hombre whom Horton recognized as Mustang Flowers, whirled by Bell's pickets.

Riding with Mustang was Mike Gans, the rancher with the cast in his flaming eye. Gans gave a shrill cry, hatred welling up, and threw himself off his horse, leaped at Horton, hand flying to his gun.

"So yuh got him," Gans bawled. "I'll kill him —"

"Get back, Gans." Bell sternly ordered Gans off. "Yuh're a member of our Association, Gans and yuh'll do as I say."

"He ruint me," grumbled Gans, but he stopped.

"He ruint us all," Bell replied. "But Horton's havin' his last say."

But Mustang Flowers took it up. The huge hombre pushed Bell aside, followed by his armed cronies. "Why palaver?" he shouted. "Gimme that rope, I'll string this skunk up myself."

"Stand back, Flowers!" ordered Bell.

Many of Bell's friends felt as Mustang did, they wanted to see Horton kicking air. Bell was shoved off by sheer weight of numbers, protests drowned in the uproar. Mustang Flowers struck Phil Horton a clip alongside the head that made Horton's ear ring, staggered him. With a curse Horton drove his iron-hard knuckles into Mustang's mouth, breaking the giant's lip against his teeth. He felt huge satisfaction as he hit Flowers a second blow in the face, before his arms were pinned by a flood of men and he went down, kicks and punches raining upon him.

The red glow of the fire lit the ominous scene. Horton felt the brutal boot of Mustang Flowers as the horsy man kicked him in the stomach. He tried to fight back but he was held down, and Flowers quickly slipped the harsh rope lariat noose about Horton's neck.

"Toss that end over," bawled Flowers. "I'll fix him."

Horton's brave heart did not quaver. He faced ignominious death with a calm certainty that he was in the right, that he was a martyr to the evil men of the Panhandle. They had murdered his father and they were going to murder him.

As he struggled to his feet, head rocking crazily from the terrible pummeling he had undergone, a hoarse shout of defiance came from his bleeding mouth. Before him was an image of a lovely woman's face, a woman with sympathetic, amber eyes — he brushed that aside, for her father had killed his, now was about to watch Phil's death —

"Flowers!"

Over the confusion of voices that incisive command penetrated to the horsy man's attention. Others heard it, and turned to see who had spoken, even as Mustang, struck by its menace, faced Jim Hatfield.

A quiet fell upon the gathering. Flowers stood frozen. Phil Horton stared curiously at the tall hombre who had stopped the lynching bee by a single word.

The flickering ruby light from the fire fell

on the long sweep of the Ranger's fighting jaw. Feet spread he stood outside the crowd, looking at Mustang. He seemed, thought Horton, to hold them in magnetic command, akin to awe. Admiration swept Horton's breast; he had seen strong men and he hoped he was one himself, but he had never seen such an hombre as this.

"Flowers," the tall jigger drawled, "I crave to know what all this is about. Yuh savvy I'm a stranger hereabouts."

"Yeah, and a damn funny one," muttered Mustang. His face was dark, jutting chin down as he glowered at the Ranger, watching a chance to catch him off guard. His hand itched to put a slug through Hatfield but he did not forget the speed of the Ranger's draw, and knew he would be first to fall when the man with the cold eyes started to shoot.

A man with a rattlesnake hatband lost his nerve; he went hysterical, whipped his pistol out. It went off but the bullet hit the dirt, for the hombre crashed dead on his face, knocked over by the sudden sheet of death from Hatfield's Colt. Before the others could go for their guns they found themselves staring into the black round eyes of two steady pistols in the Ranger's hands.

"Step over here, Horton," the big jigger ordered.

CHAPTER V
A PLEA FOR PEACE

Horton did not think of disobeying. His heart jumped as he realized he was not to die. "I'll borrow yore horse, Tazewell," Horton's savior remarked coolly. "Horton, see that bony gray — get on him and I'll be right with yuh."

"Yuh can't get away with this —" began Mustang.

"Why not?" the tall jigger asked quietly.

"Why not?" He was backing away, out of the light circle, and no one dared move for a gun. He mounted the golden sorrel but never seemed to take his gaze off the buffaloed crowd. Horton started west over the plain. The man who had snatched him from the jaws of death galloped after him. Now shots and yells rang out, lead whirled past them, but with a burst of speed they were away.

"Where to?" Horton cried, as the free wind cooled his burning face.

70

"Let's find yore friends, they oughta be around somewhere."

Horton set up a long, weird yodeling that pierced the night. An answer came from the south, and presently a band of heavily armed men rode up, greeted Horton with wild delight. Among them rode Olly Crouse, and Jeff Smith, the saturnine old herder.

"Goshamighty, Phil," Crouse yelled, "we thought you was a goner! Couldn't get near enough, though we meant to charge 'em at the last minute and die in the attempt! How in hell'd you manage to escape?"

"Thank this man," Horton replied.

The sheepmen, unkempt, beards long and clothing torn and dirty from their fugitive existence, looked upon the tall hombre who had brought their young leader out. He wore the rig of a cowman, but they accepted him, grateful for his help.

Their enemies had begun a pursuit and far-off wild shots sounded as they rode pell-mell across the rolling plains. Swinging back and forth but always bearing north, they shook off the cattlemen and slowed to rest their lathered, hard-breathing horses.

"I'm sure obliged to you," said Horton to the rugged, silent Ranger. "I don't even know your name, mister, but you saved my neck."

"Call me Jim. S'pose we head for yore camp, Horton."

All were in favor, for they were worn out. Crouse had been captured when he had ventured into Making to buy some tobacco and supplies and they had been trailing Bell and his men ever since in the rescue attempt.

Phil Horton, stalwart dark-clad figure erect in the saddle, took the lead, Hatfield jogging beside him. They rode for two hours until they came suddenly upon the canyon through which ran Rabbit Ear Creek, and not far from the hills pass whence Phil had issued to look upon the Panhandle. The cut in the flat surface was four hundred feet deep, precipitous scarps straight down to jagged rocks below. Horton swung east along the canyon till they came to the wooded hills.

The sheepmen's flying camp was here, hidden in the bushy slopes. They had some food and spare guns, blankets, in a shallow cave, and the weary men picketed their horses and flung themselves down to drink and rest. Old Jeff built a small fire in under the cliff so the smoke would not show against the moon-sky. They had slaughtered a beef and strips were fried.

Hatfield ate with them, squatted on his

haunches. Phil Horton was curious about the big man, kept watching him, wondering at his motive in having risked his life to snatch him from Marley Bell and Mustang Flowers.

When they had eaten and were smoking their pipes, Horton saw the tall, majestic jigger rise to his feet. "Gents," he drawled, "I know yuh had the wind up and yuh seem like good citizens. But I must tell yuh the pizenin' of the Panhandle range was jest what Marley says: a skunk's trick!"

Jeff Smith gave an angry snarl. "Looka here, stranger," he snarled, "yuh saved Horton, but yuh can't talk to us thataway. I —"

"Don't reach for that gun," Hatfield drawled. "Sit quiet and hear what I got to say."

"Jeff!" Horton snapped. "And all of you, do what Jim tells you!"

"Thanks," Hatfield told the young leader. "As I was sayin', that pizen business set off a nasty war that's upset the hull section."

"Jim," Horton said earnestly, "please hear me and believe what I say. No sheepmen ever laid a mite of poison on this range! That's a lie of Bell's to set people against us."

"Yuh expect me to believe that?"

"I'm tellin' you square," insisted Horton,

and a chorus of sheepmen backed him up. "I've questioned every man who brought a flock down here and not one of 'em had enough strychnine to put out such a big amount of poison. We all carry a bit to use on coyotes and other varmints, but there must've been hundreds of pounds spread 'round the Panhandle to kill so many cows."

"It wasn't strychnine," the tall jigger said. "It was arsenic."

Horton swore. "I'll pay anyone ten dollars a grain for any arsenic he can find among us! Or ever could."

"What brought you all down here?" Hatfield asked.

Phil Horton answered for them: "My father bought a grazin' lease in Oklahoma from an agent who said the cowmen were movin' south of the Red River. So did our friends. When Dad and I got here, the cattlemen claimed they weren't leavin' and the war was already on. While my father was talkin' it over with Marley Bell, Bell flared up and shot him dead."

"And," Olly Crouse added, "they druv our sheep over the cliffs or to slaughter. We're out to make 'em pay."

"Tell me," the tall jigger asked suddenly. "Did yuh happen to notice the hat of the men who sold them forged leases — for they

74

must've bin forged."

"Hat?" repeated Horton. "What you mean?"

"The band. Did them agents wear rattle-snake skin bands, trimmed with a red circle?"

Olly Crouse swore. "Come to think of it, the hombre I paid did, mister." And Phil Horton found he could agree.

Horton was exhausted, worn out by emotional strain and the hard run. He could hardly hold his eyes open, and he soon retired, rolling in his blanket.

The morning sun woke him. With the elasticity of youth, Horton had somewhat recovered from his ordeal. He had a toughness of soul that brought him through life's blows. The big jigger whom he knew as "Jim" was already up, washed in the small hill spring.

Horton ate a cold breakfast. He was smoking when one of his men, a little fellow named Morris, with a bleak, thin face, scurried up and reported that a rider was approaching, below them on the flats.

"It's a woman," Morris growled. "Looks like that Bell gal."

Phil Horton's heart jumped. "Alone?"

"Yes, sir."

As Phil started quickly south, Old Jeff

75

growled, "Look out, boy. It may be a trap to snare you."

Horton shrugged impatiently, pushed on. A small figure astride a white horse was coming from the direction of the B-in-a-Bell. The new sunlight gleamed on the strands of coppery hair escaping from beneath her Stetson. It was Lydie, and Phil Horton started out to meet her. The beat of his brain speeded and he felt cold sweat in the palms of his hands. She was even more beautiful than the picture engraved in his heart, small, so daintily made, perfect in symmetry. Her red lips were slightly parted, disclosing pearly teeth.

"No!" he muttered fiercely, "no, you fool!" He fought down the emotion that engulfed him, for she was the flesh and blood of the man who had killed his father.

The girl's face was anxious as she rode up to him. She dismounted, dropped her horse's reins and came over to the young sheepman.

"Phil Horton," she said softly, and held out a small hand to him. "I've come to talk to you." His strong, youthful figure was handsome in the morning glow; he had a fine, intelligent face, its lines stern, uncompromising now. But she knew how to soften him.

Phil Horton felt the touch of her hand on his. He was acutely aware of her loveliness, and the perfume of her hair.

"I heard about last night, Phil," she told him gently. "Father was nearly killed. I hate this war; my father's in danger every instant and it's sheer torture to my mother and me."

"Why did you come to me?" he asked, voice low.

"To beg you not to kill my father. You must realize what he means to me."

"The same as my father meant to me!"

"I understand," the girl's voice was barely a whisper, "I hate to see you so hurt. I rode to tell you that I heard one of our hands say he knew your camp was over this way so I came to warn you."

He stared at her. "Thank you." The savagery aroused in his heart was dying down; he still hated Marley Bell and the cattlemen, but the gentle young woman touched him. "I'm sorry, Lydie, that it was your father who killed mine."

"But I don't believe he did," she cried, eyes shining with conviction. "Phil, my father never fired that shot. I saw his gun myself, right after it happened, and the cylinders were full."

"Then one of his friends did it."

She shook her head. "None of them will

admit it, even now when it'd only be a feather in a cowman's hat. Someone shot your father through the window, and then knocked over the light."

"I wish I could believe that," he murmured.

Lydie reached in a pocket and brought out a white cloth. In its folds lay an empty .45 cartridge shell, blacked by carbon at the mouth. Deep marks, formed when the firing-pin had struck the rim, could plainly be seen in the clear light.

"I picked this up in the room where your father died. It had rolled under a chair —" She broke off, turning.

"I'd like to see that shell, ma'am!"

Phil Horton looked around, saw the tall jigger, his savior. "Jim! You gave us a start. Meet Miss Lydie Bell."

Hatfield bowed gravely. "Could I have a look at that cartridge, Miss Lydie?"

She held it out to him. He took it, turning it over and over, rugged face keen.

"Off center," Phil Horton heard him grunt. Phil knew that to an expert's eyes a discharged cartridge case often tells a whole story. Then he began to wonder how much of their talk the tall hombre had overheard. Lydie rose.

"I must get back, before I'm missed. Phil,

I'm going to try to get my father to agree to a truce, so that this war can be settled. Will you promise to hold your men till you hear from me?"

"A good idea," agreed Hatfield. "Miss Lydie, tell yore father the sheepmen didn't spread that pizen."

"I'll do that. You promise, then, Phil?"

Phil Horton drew in a deep breath of the warm, scented air. It was difficult to change his viewpoint, which was that the cattlemen of the Panhandle were murderous devils; he could not quench all his hatred in one moment. But both Hatfield and Lydie he admired, and they exerted a powerful sway over the young sheepman chief, despite Phil's own strong nature. He was not, at heart, a killer, he had been fighting for what he thought was right, and to punish the slayer of his father.

The Ranger supplied the finishing argument that convinced Horton: "If," he said "yuh're tellin' the truth 'bout not layin' that pizen, Phil, mebbe Bell's innocent of yore dad's murder."

"That's true," said Horton. "All right — I promise. I'll hold my men till I hear from you, Lydie. Will you send me word or do you want me to come to the ranch?"

"I'll send you a message," she replied.

She smiled as she gave him her hand. He helped her mount, his spirit lifted. He watched her gallop toward home, across the gray-brown plain.

When he could no longer see her, he turned back to the tall jigger. Hatfield had his golden horse saddled up and was preparing to mount. "Where you goin'?" asked Horton.

"West."

"How far, Jim? You know the Comanches are out. We saw a war party in the distance a couple of days ago."

"I'm headin' thataway."

"Not alone? We'll go with you."

Hatfield shook his head. "I got to move fast. Lie low and yuh'll hear from me." He nodded, and Goldy lined out across the undulating prairie. Phil Horton watched the departure with deep regret. He liked the big man and would have enjoyed staying in his company. As he finally swung to return to camp, he saw Olly Crouse coming rapidly to meet him.

"Jeff says there's a passel of cowboys headin' our way, Phil. We'll hafta fight."

Horton set his strong chin and walked to the gathering. The sheepmen were carefully checking rifles and pistols, filling their pockets with spare bullets. As he looked around at the fierce, determined faces of his followers, Horton thought that sometimes it is easier to fight than not to fight.

"We're fadin', boys," he growled.

"What!" exclaimed Old Jeff. "Why, we kin knock off a dozen 'fore they reach the hills!"

A chorus of approbation backed up the old herder. Horton scowled. He ran his eyes around the circle, catching each man's gaze. He spoke deliberately.

"Get your horses," he ordered, "and we'll fade back across the creek."

They obeyed but they didn't like it. Jeff, who had loved David Horton as a son, cursed and grumbled, threatening rebellion.

But Horton was determined to hold their furious passions in control. A new, wild hope had come to him, a hope he knew could never be fulfilled if Marley Bell were assassinated by a sheepman. His former conviction that the ranchers of the Panhandle were responsible for his father's death was shaken, and he swore to discover the truth.

They swung into their saddles, ragged in nondescript costumes, overalls or corduroys, old caps or felts faded by the sun. Keen-eyed hombres coming swiftly toward them spied their movements on the brushy slopes. Whoops rose and rifle bullets began to plop into the stony dirt.

"They'll find our camp," Old Jeff growled, red-eyed with fury. "Let's stay and have it out. We can knock off the hull bunch if we lie up here in these rocks."

"Ride," snapped Phil Horton. Shortly after that they began to retreat north through the pass.

"I'll hafta get in touch with her later," Horton muttered to himself as they rode, "or else, she won't know where to find me." He decided, as soon as he had shaken off the cowboys and the way was clear, that he would go to the Bell ranch, find Lydie, since now she might not be able to locate him.

Far to the west, Horton's friend Jim was a faint dust-roll on the horizon, swiftly headed toward the red terrors of the plains, the Comanches.

CHAPTER VI
THE RED RAIDERS

Suspicion burned Jim Hatfield's keen brain. From what he had uncovered he had come to believe that the wholesale poisoning of the range had been done by someone other than Horton's sheepmen. Every sign pointed to another far more sinister, powerful agency. The motive of this menacing, engulfing enemy, against which he matched his wits and brawn, was still obscure to him but he meant to discover it, try to balk it — if he was not killed.

Hatfield was certain that the men who wore the rattlesnake hatbands, among them Mustang Flowers and his tough crew, would not work simply for pleasure. There must be profit in it for them, and a large stake, to employ such a great number. There were, Hatfield deduced, so many of them in the Panhandle that they wore the headbands so as to recognize one another.

The territory he must cover was vast,

hundreds of miles in extent, involving many counties. In it lived thousands of decent citizens, panic-stricken by the Indian raids, by the seemingly wide-spread sheep-cattle war, wild bullets and poison endangering their lives. They had the right of protection, and Texas must offer it.

The wind-rustled, dry grasses, interspersed with mesquite thickets, with giant cacti, covered the rolling land ocean; appalling numbers of steer carcasses, picked of meat by buzzards and coyotes, bleached in the brilliant sunlight. The range seemed deserted, save for a smoke mist here and there, way off, marking a ranch or a settler's home.

Goldy held his tireless pace westward. Hatfield, aware of the great strength of the hidden enemy he was fighting, rode through the day; the sun was in his face as he came to the northeastern margin of the Staked Plain, the Llano Estacado. The gray-green eyes swept its tremendous reaches.

"She's shore big," he mused, talking to the sorrel. For hundreds of miles the dry table land, sered by a burning sun, dotted with skulls of men and beasts, spread before him. A man might wander on it until he dropped dead, so unchanging was its aspect; Hatfield was aware that long ago the Spanish missionary padres, carrying the Light into the wilderness, had been forced to set up buffalo skulls on stakes to mark a trail so they should not lose themselves in the unbounded spaces.

To the north, brush-covered hills broke the monotony of flatness. As his desert-trained eyes swept that way he caught a sudden flash in the sky, answered by another beyond to the west. Into the brittle blue of the heavens rose a smoke-puff, as sharply outlined as a pencil sketch. Signals, he decided, of the Comanches. They must have seen him.

He turned Goldy north, heading for the hills, into the very jaws of a torture death, but he did not falter. The red raiders, lurking in the foothills, could dash down through Northwest Texas or retreat across the State line into New Mexico if too large a force appeared against them.

Jagged rocks blocked the way, but he found a trail winding through. As he started into this sinuous passage, a man with a cruel face, crowned by a Stetson with rattlesnake band dotted with a vermilion circle, rose up at his left, rifle flying to his shoulder to cover the Ranger.

Goldy snorted and reared at this sudden apparition. Hatfield left his saddle as his hat

85

flew from his head, knocked off by the long bullet snapping through the crown. He fired as his feet jolted to earth, at the snarling face of the drygulcher. His accurate pistol flamed true, and the hombre slumped out of sight in his rock nest.

The Ranger quickly looked round. This fellow was plainly an outpost. The hatband told him the Comanches must be friendly with members of that gang invading the Northwest.

He crawled to the rocks, gun ready, but the man wasn't playing possum. Hatfield's shot had smashed through his brain.

Goldy snorted and pawed the stones in frantic warning. The Ranger was determined to stop the Indians if it could be done; an idea flashed through him. Quickly he removed the dead man's Stetson, with its snake band, and strapped it on his own head. He tossed his own punctured hat behind the rocks where the drygulcher lay, and remounted, long jaw drawn up by the tight chinstrap of the black Stetson with its distinctive badge.

He had climbed but a few hundred yards when Goldy sniffed at the hot air, quivered. "Indians!" the sorrel told Hatfield as plainly as though he spoke.

The tip of an eagle feather showed over a

red rock. A dozen rifle barrels covered the Ranger, the setting sun glinting on the burnished new steel, and a gruff challenge hailed him:

"Pull up, fella!"

Jim Hatfield calmly looked up into the dark, savage face of the hombre who had tried to pick off John Farnsworth at the Making mass meeting.

He knew what a gamble he was taking; he was depending on the rattlesnake hatband to see him through.

"Howdy," he drawled, no worry in his voice. "Jest took a couple of shots at a jackrabbit."

The hatband, the Ranger's unruffled demeanor, did the trick. The savage hombre's eyes fixed on the badge — the sand-colored hat pulled down to his flaming black eyes was decorated in the same fashion. He came down onto the trail, half a dozen Comanche braves slipping through the rocks with him, iron-muscled, sinewy bodies like so many copperheads.

Hatfield's gaze swept them. They were naked save for a skin strip, but they were well armed with ammunition belts of new canvas, the loops filled with shining cartridges, and scalping knives at the waist. The coarse, black hair of each brave was bound by a strip of snake skin, one or two eagle feathers, denoting the number of enemies killed in battle, rising from it. Bronzed, fierce faces, high-cheeked, smeared to gargoyle masks by vermilion war paint. Dark eyes fixed the Texas Ranger's mighty figure.

"Young men," mused Hatfield — he saw no elders, no great chiefs. Every Comanche carried a new rifle.

He had taken a long chance, riding in this way, but he had won. They obeyed the commands of the white man with the rattlesnake hatband. Hatfield regarded him closely, he wore thorn-scratched black chaps, boots with spur attachers; his face was cruel as a panther's, deep-black, slit eyes, a sneering lip and curved beak over a tiny mustache that twitched as he spoke.

"Where yuh from, hombre?"

"Amarillo," answered Hatfield, on guard. He had felt forced to make this dangerous play; only by such bold moves could he hope to cover the vast Panhandle in time to save Texas.

His answer seemed satisfactory. "How's things there? They plenty panicked?"

"Shore. I rode around by Making and they're fussed, too."

"Good. The boss expected trouble there,

it's the hub, that's why he's made his headquarters there. Well, we're all ready to start at dawn tomorrow, the Injuns're itchin' for that south raid. The big drive is still set for Friday, ain't it? No change?"

Hatfield was coolly feeling his way, playing his cards as they came up. So Making was where the "boss" had his headquarters! And he must try to stop the proposed raid —

"I got a message," he drawled. "That's why I rode here. The Boss wants that raid held up a day or two."

"What!" the other snarled. "Why, he must've gone loco! Why hold back? I got these red devils primed for hell!"

The Ranger slung a long leg around his saddle horn as Goldy stamped uneasily, hating the Indian odor. "The Boss ain't ready yet. Something's come up!"

"Huh!" The savage hombre spat angrily. "Now listen — say, what's yore handle?"

"Jim Harrison."

"Mine's Blackie Pruitt. Since yuh bring sech orders, relay 'em to the Injuns. C'mon."

Blackie strolled off. Horses waited nearby in the next dip, and mounting, they rode upward for a mile, coming to a small flat where an Indian camp stood. A hundred braves lounged about, sprang up as the whites appeared. Again the Ranger noted that these Comanches were young, most wearing one feather. He had anticipated meeting a chief or two who might know him, for he had dealt with these riders of the plains in previous campaigns, could converse fluently in sign language and Comanche.

When Blackie told the braves that the raid was postponed, rumblings of discontent rose. "You tell 'em," Blackie said.

Jim Hatfield rose, facing the savage gathering. Countenances imperturbable, yet the dark eyes shone as the Indians looked on the great Ranger, admiration for a fighting man sweeping them.

"Comanches of the Staked Plain," Hatfield began slowly, with great dignity he knew the Indians demanded, "have you not sworn to obey the orders of the Men with the Snake Hats?"

It seemed they had sworn obedience but were heated for the raid south. Had they not, asked their spokesman, been promised that the Texas Panhandle would be restored to them if they allied themselves with these powerful strangers? The settlers had encroached on their hunting grounds and several Comanches been shot from ambush by whites.

Without seeming to ask information, Hatfield craftily drew them out. He learned the reason for the absence of the chiefs and elders. The latter looked askance at the new war; they had tried it too often in the past and been crushingly defeated by the Texas Rangers. But the Rattlesnakes had bribed the youths, started them on their flaming raids.

As they parleyed darkness fell. The red glow of camp-fires lit the hollow. The Comanches drew apart to talk among themselves. Blackie Pruitt tossed some food to Hatfield, and the two whites squatted by a fire.

"Workin' these red devils is some job," growled Blackie. "They're like kids. I got sick of 'em and took a run to Smithtown t'other day for a spree. They're scairt silly there, so near the Injuns. I don't s'pose yuh heard of my play at Making, did yuh? I hafta laugh at my own nerve sometimes!"

Hatfield, jaws working in a strip of jerked beef, shook his head. "No. I wasn't there."

"It worked swell. Yuh gotta hand it to the Guvnor, he knows how to sway a crowd. Say, I forgot to ask: what's yore number? Yuh must have plenty brains, like me, since yuh know the big boss."

91

Hatfield had to reply. "Sixty-seven," he answered.

The fire shone ruby-red in Blackie Pruitt's savage eyes. Pruitt was silent for a moment, chewing on his beef. "Yuh savvy," he said softly, "I missed Farnsworth that time, but I'll get the dawg!"

Hatfield grunted. Under long-lashed lids he watched Blackie, who drawled, "Yuh work with Morgan at Amarillo?"

Was Blackie suspicious or was he still fooled by the Ranger's sang-froid and the snake badge? Had that number been right? The Ranger was not equipped with the inside knowledge to keep on with his deception, now Blackie had started on this tack.

Pruitt made no inimical move. Hatfield kept an eye on the savage hombre; Goldy stood, saddled and ready, a few yards off in the shadows; he could retreat, fight his way off if he was forced to do so.

"I better put more wood on the fire," Blackie remarked. He shifted, grabbing up a heavy log and raising it, he whirled suddenly, face a mask of suspicious hatred, bringing the stick around in a vicious arc that ended at Hatfield's head. The blow cracked with a terrible thud that set the Ranger's smashed ear bleeding, sent him sideward off balance. With a hot curse

Blackie kicked red-hot embers into the Ranger's eyes.

"Yuh damn lyin' spy," shrieked Pruitt, and his hand flashed to his gun.

Hatfield acted with the speed of light; his eyes stung furiously from the hot coals but it was life or death and his blue-steel Colt jerked from its supple oiled holster, hammer coming back under his thumb. Blackie's big pistol roared a flash of yellow flame, through the rising smoke. Hatfield's thumb rose.

A devastating pain, blinding light, smashed the Lone Wolf's brain; he jerked backward, head banging on a stone. He was aware that Pruitt had paused, right in front of the fire, as though suddenly paralyzed. He tried to come back, to finish the fight, but in a strange half-consciousness, a nightmare illusion, he was unable to move a muscle. Pruitt toppled, falling on the embers. A smell of singed cloth and flesh rose in the smoky air.

When Jim Hatfield recovered himself he was on the jolting saddle of a horse. Shoots of anguish stung his brain. In the moonlight the sinister shapes of the naked Comanches surrounded him on their hairy mustangs. He did not show he was awake, but kept his eyes closed, he was not tied up, so he decided to make a sudden leap in order to escape.

The moon was high in the sky when they stopped. They had come west through the broken foothills, and entered a large camp which woke to life, dogs yelping, squaws running forth, armed braves appearing from tepees. A fire, piled with dry twigs, flamed high, lighting the scene with a ruddy glow. A Comanche superchief, a full headdress of eagle feathers trailing the ground, stalked forth to face the young braves who had brought in the Ranger. He was a majestic figure, a long face set with stern lines, fiery eyes.

Hatfield recognized him. It was Chief Long Lance, head of the Comanche nation. With him the Texas Rangers, after a long, bloody war, had concluded a treaty of peace.

There was now no opportunity to escape. Hatfield husbanded his power and wits, shocked brain recovering — Pruitt's bullet had driven a deep gash in his scalp, bruised the skull. No doubt, thought the Ranger, one of his answers, perhaps his number, had aroused Blackie's suspicions, and, drawing him out, he had come upon sure proof that Hatfield was an impostor.

He played possum, though the Indians did not seem unfriendly. He was lifted from

Goldy's back and propped against a stone, while Long Lance, arms folded, chin high, looked him over. The great chief swung on the crowd of young braves, who were puzzled. "I have told you they would come," Long Lance said in Comanche. "You are fools."

"But — he wore a Rattlesnake hat! And yet he fought and killed the commissioner!"

Long Lance grunted. He stooped to skin back one of Hatfield's eyelids. "Luckily for you he's not dead. He is the craftiest, strongest warrior of the Rangers. Put him on his horse and I will take him to Singing Bear, our great medicine man."

Hatfield was lifted back on Goldy. Long Lance mounted a buckskin, and leading the sorrel, left the big camp. Once out of hearing, the Ranger softly spoke the chief's name and Long Lance turned, wrinkled face staring as Hatfield righted himself, sagging in his seat.

"Long Lance," said the Ranger gravely, "your braves have broken the Treaty." He spoke in Comanche.

"I could not hold them," shrugged the chief. "I told them they were fools but the Rattlesnake man bribed them. But why are you wearing that badge?"

"A ruse of war." Hatfield was shaken, his

head felt as though it was coming off.

They made a mile through wild, dry hills. A black hole yawned in the side of a rock-crusted cliff. "Singing Bear's cave," grunted Long Lance. "He has kept us here a month while he communes with the great spirit who gives him power." At the chief's hail a weird figure crawled forth, an Indian in a bear's head, grizzly claws clanking on his withered breast. "Singing Bear brings back the dead to life," Long Lance said solemnly. "He will heal you."

From the depths of the cavern issued a hollow groan. "What's that?" muttered Hatfield, as the blood-chilling sound came again.

"That is Singing Bear's spirit guide, which keeps us here."

The medicine man would not let them enter his den. He retired, but emerged again. He smeared a salve on Hatfield's aching wound, chanting as he applied it. The salve stung like liquid fire. The Ranger swallowed hand-rolled green pellets Singing Bear forced on him. After a minute the worst pain eased and his eyelids grew so heavy he could no longer hold them open.

Dawn roused him from his strange stupor. Long Lance squatted at his head, and he lay in the chief's own tepee. Squaws brought him nourishing broth and renewed power surged through his great frame. His scalp was stiff and sore to the touch but the pain had left.

An hour later he rode out of Long Lance's camp. The chief went with him for a mile. "You will hear from me," the Ranger promised. The chief raised a long arm in salute.

When he reached the plains, Hatfield galloped the golden sorrel southeast. He passed the blackened remains of three shanties where settlers had grouped; later he saw in the distance one of the big Panhandle ranches. At noon the buildings of a small town rose on the horizon and he headed for it.

Smithtown's single street stretched north and south on the grassy flats, sod houses, raw, unpainted shacks leaning toward each other under the blazing copper sun. A crowd of citizens listened to a shouted speech of a man who stood up in a buckboard wagon. Pulling up on the outskirts, the Ranger regarded the speaker. It was John Farnsworth, the orator he had heard in Making.

"What must we do to save ourselves, citizens of the Panhandle?" bellowed Farnsworth. "Band together and stop the violence of the feudal ranchers, drive back the red raiders of the Staked Plain!" As his eyes swept the gathering in the central plaza, they fell on the mounted Ranger, visible over the heads of the throng. Farnsworth faltered, but went on.

Men with rattlesnake bands were sprinkled through the crowd. Farnsworth concluded his fiery talk to loud cheers and handclapping, climbed down, men pushing about him to congratulate him.

A huge figure hustled from a saloon. It was Mustang Flowers, and with him several of his gunfighters. Vermilion circles gleamed in the bright light. Flowers listened to the words of a man from the crowd who slipped up to him; galvanized to action, Flowers uttered a hoarse shout, gun flashing out as he started for Hatfield, men hurriedly closing in.

The Lone Wolf, in his perilous scanning of the field, had seen enough to draw his conclusion. Throughout the great extent of the Panhandle the panic had been spread by the threat of the Indians, the sheep-cattle war; in other towns the citizens would be demanding action as in Making and Smithtown. He knew he faced a huge, welded organization of evil men, that he must gather quickly a fighting force in an attempt to circumvent them.

It was Jim Hatfield's method, once certain of his ground, to go direct to the heart of an evil. Blackie Pruitt, before his suspicion had flared, had said the boss of this devilish crew made headquarters at Making City, and Hatfield was on his way back there.

Mustang Flowers howled, "Bandit — bandit!" as Goldy lined out. Bullets from his enemies whirled after the flying Ranger, and he swung in his saddle, eyes cold with an icy fury, as a dozen of them, egged on by the giant Flowers, mounted in pursuit. Out on the plain, away from the citizens, Hatfield's Colts began to spit death, the swift legs of the golden sorrel rapidly increasing the space between them.

Making lay east, where the "Governor" Blackie Pruitt had mentioned, issued his murderous orders, that had disrupted life in the Panhandle. He would ferret out the leaders behind the criminal array. The blast of his pistols slowed Mustang and his men down; one yelped, gripping his shoulder, falling out of line.

Darkness had fallen when Jim Hatfield hit Making City, swinging into Main Street from the north, heading for Tazewell's. Goldy stepped along, dust thick on his wet, tawny hide. The tall rider's gray-green eyes never were quiet; they roved with the restlessness of the trained wilderness scout who is eternally vigilant, who must watch every angle for lurking death. First right, then to the left, now and then turning his head to make sure he was not trailed, Hatfield proceeded.

As the Lone Wolf broke out into the light lane between buildings, an owl on the right flank gave an eerie hoot; another replied down the road. The soft cries were almost lost in the town's hum, but Hatfield was instantly suspicious, ears and eyes, every sense alert. He knew the call of birds and animals, including owls, and the first cry had a slightly rusty note. Besides, owls do not favor a noisy settlement.

The Ranger yanked Goldy's rein, and the quick movement saved him as a bullet spanged past his head, slapping into a house wall beyond. A second burned the flesh of his left arm. Red-yellow blares showed as the guns spat death his way. Goldy spurted for a shadowed space, Hatfield's swift Colt booming a reply at the flashes. A sharp yip of pain rang out.

Other attackers were hurrying up. The Ranger cut between two houses, swung south along the narrow alley. A pistol flashed close at hand, but the golden sorrel's sharp hoofs struck down the gunman, whose snakeband hat flew off as he fell, writhing behind them in the dirt.

"Layin' for us, Goldy," the Ranger grunted.

Fierce-faced enemies came dashing through after him. His Colts cleared a way, forcing them to cover. He skirted barns and sheds, tin-can piles thrown from back doors of the Main Street homes. He cut through an opening, crossed the plaza and headed south, coming around to Tazewell's from that direction. Leaving Goldy hidden in a shed, he went silently on foot toward the trapper's.

He slid from shadow to shadow, crouched in the shelter of a high board fence. He knew he was in the right place from the acrid odor of hides on the warm air.

Hatfield's eyes swept the dark lines of the warehouse. A man's figure stood outlined against a corner, framed in front of light from the street. Then he saw a second sentinel shift, slowly walking the side toward him. The warehouse, too, was covered.

Hatfield wanted Tazewell's help in planning his attack on the criminal horde which had sunk its fangs deep into the bleeding flesh of Texas. In his work for his beloved state he had faced powerful combinations, by his strength of body and brain he had

101

overcome them.

Death was his saddle-mate when he rode the Rio Grande; he had solved the black mystery of the Border Pack, matched his wits against the elusive Ghost Rider. He had cleared the Texas Trail when ghouls snatched men to sell their corpses for gold. But the task before him now was to save Texas herself from disintegration, to stop a rapidly growing civil war. The creepers of this ranged over hundreds of square miles. He was closing in, feeling a way, picking up lines that might finally lead him to the instigator of the deadly plot.

Only death could stop the Lone Wolf. Sometimes an evil power was too great to smash; a bullet in the right place would mean that Texas died, too. Obsessed by the knowledge he must make haste, hurry, as McDowell had warned, he knew that he dared not lose a single hour.

The yard at the rear of Tazewell's was deep in shadows, sheds and drying-racks cutting off light beams. Foot by foot, a shadow himself, Hatfield crept closer and closer to the back door. Squatted behind a hogshead that caught rainwater from a long roof, a sentry's soft tread reached his ear, and a moment later the hombre swung the turn. A blast from the man's double-barreled shotgun would bring the whole crew upon him.

The Ranger waited, as the guard swung and came back. At the corner he met another man patrolling the adjoining side. "See anything, Ben?" mumbled the second guard.

"Nope, Lefty," Ben replied. "Yuh hear that shootin' up above?"

"Yeah," Lefty said gruffly. "Mebbe they caught him."

They parted, to resume their beats. Hatfield rose and walked boldly across the open space toward Ben, who carried his shotgun muzzle down across his arm.

"Ben!" the Ranger called softly.

Hearing his name the hombre faced him, did not challenge or fire. Slouched, the snakeband hat shading his features, Hatfield was upon him.

"Mustang says to keep a tight watch, Ben," he drawled. That instant's hesitation, caused by his use of Ben's name, gave the Lone Wolf his chance. A long hand snaked out, gripped Ben's throat with a clutch of a powerful vise, crushing the cartilege of the sentry's neck, stopping his outcry.

Ben's instinct, at the terrible grip that shut off all his wind in sickening sensation, was to raise his hands to claw at the Ranger's

103

wrists. Hatfield's left hand brushed the shotgun from his loosened hold. The tall Ranger gripped Ben, a spurred boot tripping the guard. The man crashed, and Hatfield's knee drove into his belly. It was only instants until Hatfield, toting the unconscious Ben, was inside the warehouse, the door closed behind him. He paused in the dark storeroom to gag and tie his captive, and shoved him under a pile of cowhides.

A thin ribbon of yellow light showed at Tazewell's room. Hatfield crossed swiftly, shoved in the door. Virgil Tazewell lay on his bunk, reading a paper; the slight creak of the portal startled him and he swung, eyes wide, hand starting for the holstered gun that hung on a chair back.

"Easy, Tazewell," Hatfield cautioned. "It's Jim."

Chapter VII
The Shooting Match

Jim Hatfield heard the hissing intake of the trapper's breath. "Hatfield! Glad to see you. Been worried 'bout you. What've you found?"

"A lot. Now I ain't got much time to palaver, but I want you to get up a shootin' match tomorrow afternoon. Be certain Mustang Flowers and Marley Bell take part. Can yuh arrange it?"

Tazewell stared at him, forehead puzzled lines. "What's your idee?"

"I got to prove, and quick, it wasn't Marley Bell who kilt David Horton. I need them ranchers and I can use the sheepmen too."

"But — Marley Bell *did* shoot Horton!"

Hatfield shook his head. "I believe diff'rent. That murder was done to prevent any truce between the cowmen and the sheepherders, to further the war. I want yuh to pick up and mark the shells from every man's gun tomorrow."

Tazewell shrugged, nodded. "Whatever you say, Jim." His eyes swept the tall Lone Wolf, took in the wounds, the white ring about the set lips. "You've had a tough time," he muttered. "Stay here, I'll shake you up some grub and a drink."

"No time. Watch yourself, Tazewell. They got sentries 'round yore warehouse. I run into 'em jest now when I come in."

Tazewell nodded, bit his lip. "I'm safe enough."

"Yeah, yuh got plenty of friends in the Panhandle. They're usin' you as a bait to take me, I s'pose, but jest the same be careful. Adios, then — till the shootin' bee tomorrow."

The Lone Wolf nodded, slipped from the room, faded into the darkness. He crossed to where he had left the trussed Ben, dragged the now squirming captive to the exit. Softly he opened the door an inch. The coast looked clear; with Ben, eyes rolling white with fear, the Ranger went silently into the shadows.

Lefty, the tall sentry from the other wall, jumped from the corner with a high pitched curse. He had come back, failed to meet Ben, and was aroused.

"Who's that?" he asked sharply, seeing the

thick bulk of Hatfield holding up Ben. "That yuh, Ben?" As Hatfield failed to reply for an instant, Lefty's nervous trigger finger contracted. Ben, in Hatfield's grip, jerked violently, began to twitch, for Lefty's hasty slug drilled his friend. Hatfield felt the warm life blood spurt from Ben's chest.

More men were yelling, running toward them. Hatfield dropped Ben, crouching as he made his draw. A bullet snapped at his Stetson crown; his firing-pin struck and Lefty took the slug in the stomach, doubling up like a jack-knife.

Hatfield jumped away, crossed the yard, the rap of lead close to him in the shed wall. He doubled back along the high fence. Beyond loomed the bulk of Frank Ulman's warehouse; Ulman was the man who had for a song, taken in thousands of cattle hides from the poisoned stock of the Panhandle.

A window was close at hand, giving into Ulman's. The place was dark. Out of sight for the moment, Hatfield coolly tried the sash, and it raised under his hand. He climbed in, shut the window, crouched in the darkness. Men hurried past the glass, not looking in.

The Ranger stuck out his hand, felt a bale of hides. The odor was strong. He made his way around, and the warehouse was full of them. Cupping his palm he struck a match. By the yellow flare he examined the inner sides of several cowhides. He repeated this at several different spots. There were grains of white arsenic clinging to them.

A latch snapped to the right and he crouched down between two high bales. "Light that lamp!" a gruff voice ordered.

It was Mustang Flowers. Peering out, the Ranger saw the giant gunman, and a man in black stooping over a lantern. The flame burned up on the wick, chimney clicking down. The hombre with Flowers was Frank Ulman, the sallow-faced dealer. They came through the narrow aisles, inspecting the hides.

"Look," Flowers growled, "yuh got to brush the arsenic out of them skins, Ulman. That's somethin' we overlooked. Seems it works into the hide. Better ship these pronto and collect the money; my boys got to have their pay reg'lar."

"I'm shippin' fast as I can," Ulman replied shortly. "Some of those dealers I contracted with outside will go bust on this market and refuse to pay."

"Look, Guv'nor," Mustang told him sardonically, "most of 'em'll pay and swaller their losses. A contract's a contract and these was signed at the price before the market broke. The ranchers kept theirs, didn't they?"

"They had to; nothing else to do."

"Things'll hum from now on," Flowers gloated. "Pruitt started the Comanches south at dawn this mornin'. It'll be the finishin' touch, Ulman. Yuh comin' uptown?"

"Yeah. Guess it's time."

A light showed at the window through which the Ranger had come. A sharp tap sounded on the glass, and Mustang Flowers hurried over, threw up the sash. "What's up?" he demanded.

"That big jigger jest shot Ben and wounded Lefty! He —"

Flowers suddenly gave a hot curse. His gunmen were gathering about the window.

"Blood!" Mustang said sharply. "Blood on the sill, wet!"

Flowers whirled, gun out, cocked. "Throw a circle round the house, boys, pronto! Some of you come in."

The Ranger pushed down among the smelly hides, realizing what had happened. Blood off Ben, when he had him close, had soaked Hatfield's clothes and left smears on the sill when he had climbed through the window.

Mustang acted fast, drawing the net about the warehouse. Every instant it closed tighter — he dared not wait. Then Hatfield came up shooting, and Flowers uttered a stentorian shout as he recognized the tall jigger.

"There he is. Get him!" Mustang's bellow filled the warehouse. Ulman, lantern high, stood between Hatfield and Flowers. Men in the window opened up with a melody of death, guns blasting through the big room. Jim Hatfield's first slug smashed the lantern, spattering the sallow Ulman's face and eyes with hot glass fragments. The dealer screamed, fell to the floor, the lantern rolling away, spilling oil that took fire.

Flowers ducked, firing hurriedly at the spot where he had glimpsed his foe. Confused yells rose with the shooting. Hatfield could see the rectangle of the window, bunched with men and his Colts tore through, the gun-fighters who took his lead screeching in anguish.

The Lone Wolf leaped away, on top of the rustling, yielding bales of hides. The other side was shadowed, as the lantern oil smokily burned on the board floor. To his left loomed the open door and he jumped toward it. Colts up, angled to right and left. His boots were spread in fighting stance.

Men dashed in from both sides. His bullets smashed the gunmen, rattled them, stopped their charge; he was moving again as a slug burned his back, stinging with horrid agony. He forced on, lead thick about him, ripping his clothes and skin. He vaulted the high fence, swung to empty a pistol at his enemies. Bullets drilled the fence, drove through carrying jagged splinters with them.

He slid around Tazewell's and cut up the lane behind Main Street. Citizens, alarmed by the heavy shooting, were running toward the warehouse. Looking back he saw a red glow that was the doorway of Ulman's.

He found a large barn, entered and climbed to a mow. Hidden in the soft, fragrant hay, the Ranger made himself comfortable, planning for the morrow.

Two hours later a rider on a lathered horse flogged from the south, crossed the railroad tracks into Making City. He passed Tazewell's and did not pause; the odor of smoke hung heavy on the breeze. Ulman's, too, was dark. The rider wore a rattlesnake band, dotted by a vermilion circle, on his hat.

The newcomer left his horse at a hitchrack and proceeded afoot, cutting between buildings to the rear lane. At the door of a square brown house he was challenged, gave a satisfactory reply, and was admitted to a room lit by a single lamp, wick turned down, giving off a dim illumination.

Inside waited several others, seated about a table, some were travel-stained, faces grim under the snake-trimmed Stetsons. Tobacco smoke clouded up against the low ceiling.

A step sounded in the hall, and a man in a dark cloak, mask drawn up over his features, entered. A murmur of awe rustled through the gathering. He slumped in a chair, and the lamp cast his shadow hugely grotesque on the wall, a vagary of distortion giving it the outline of a vulture. Chin on breast, glowing eyes alone visible, he swept the cruel faces of his henchmen, who waited his pleasure.

He gave a short nod, at the man who had come from the south. "Things were linin' up swell, Guv'nor," the hombre reported. "But what the hell happened to the Comanches!"

"What?" snarled the governor. "They began their raid this morning, didn't they?"

"No, sir, nary hide nor hair showed. Folks in Amarillo and the district figger the Injuns 've retreated."

Hot curses spat from the muffled lips of the leader. "Everything's planned for Friday. The mass meeting, delegates from every county are coming. It's timed to the instant! But I must have unanswerable arguments and now —"

A hurried, heavy tread shook the floor, as a giant figure burst into the room. "Hey, Jarvis!"

The governor slammed a fist on the table, and his men jumped. "You fool! Don't use that name here."

"Sorry, but I jest got word that after we left Smithtown a line rider toted in Blackie Pruitt's corpse. He says the Comanches dumped it on the range, with a daid rattlesnake looped around his neck!"

Widening eyes fixed the governor, awaiting his reaction. When he spoke, his voice made them squirm uncomfortably. The tone was icy but the repressed fury was vicious with menace.

"One man has done this! One man, I tell you. The man who snatched Horton, and has nearly brought about a truce. He was in Smithtown, no doubt returning after killing our agent, Pruitt. I pay you, hundreds of you; yet you allow a single man to balk me! He must die at once!"

"He's a right salty fighter, Guv'nor," the big man with the horse face growled defensively. "I had plenty hombres set to drygulch him, but he's slippery as an eel and quick as light. Besides him bein' a Ranger, we gotta be keerful who sees us finish him."

"Don't try to excuse yourself. I'll patch

up the damage you've let this spy do. We make our play Friday and neither hell nor high water 'll stop me."

"S'posin' the cattlemen try to bust it up?"

"They won't. I'll make sure they sign no truce with Horton. They must be kept busy till we're in full control. Send Slim Roberts to me here first thing tomorrow."

"What's yore idee?" asked the giant curiously.

The governor shrugged. "I am a master at disguise," he replied.

"Yeah, that's true. But what's that gotta do with Marley Bell and Horton? Bell's daughter's sweet on Horton and him on her and they're fightin' for peace!"

The governor's words hissed through clenched teeth: "When I've finished with her not even a dog will want to look at her face!"

"Acid?" growled the big man, a horrified note in his voice.

The burning eyes glowered his way. "Are you going soft?" he asked, a note of disgust in his voice.

The giant backed down. After a while another man cleared his throat and asked softly, "What yuh want us to do, guv'nor?"

"All of you ride back to your districts and work on as you've been instructed. Be sure your county delegates come to the Making mass meeting Friday. We must strike, and strike fast."

He pushed back his chair, rose, swept the circle with a soul-searing glance, stalked out.

At 3 P.M. Jim Hatfield checked his blue-steel Colts and strolled across Making plaza, north along Main Street. The saloons were deserted, and the sidewalks empty too. Everybody was at the shooting match, held in the big open space at the north end.

Already sharp gun-fire rose on the warm air. The tall Ranger paused near the spot where Blackie Pruitt had made his escape the day Farnsworth had been wounded while making his speech. His gray-green eyes swept the great crowd of people. The majority were honest citizens, worried and harassed by the fear of the Indians and the slump brought on by the sheep-cattle war. They were happy to have a chance to forget their troubles for the moment, watching the contest of skill at the targets. Men wearing the snakeskin hatbands moved among the people.

"Figger they won't dare try to murder me in front of the crowd," mused Hatfield. Keeping in the background he looked over the layout. There were plenty of horses standing about and if he was forced he

115

could make cover as Blackie Pruitt had and escape.

A rectangular space a hundred yards long had been roped off. At the sides spectators stood or sat in wagons. The east end, where the targets were set on thick butts, was clear. Virgil Tazewell's lean figure, in buckskin, Hatfield regarded with deep interest. Tazewell, a very popular, well-known person in the Panhandle, was an official. Now and then, as a contestant emptied his warm six-shooter of shells, Tazewell would stoop, pick them up, unostentatiously slip them into his pockets.

The mayor of Making, Ben Decker, was a judge, and a heavy-set hombre, with an uneven brown mustache, a star on his brown vest, sat with Decker. That was Sheriff Dog Wilson. Wilson looked stolidly substantial and earnest, though, Hatfield decided, none too clever. The sheriff's blue jowls worked as he chewed at his tobacco cud.

Marley Bell was firing now. The small rancher chief was an expert shot. Most Panhandle citizens prided themselves on their marksmanship; a shooting match such as this was keenly fascinating, and bets were laid on the champions.

Mustang Flowers followed Bell, a complacent smirk on his horsy face. The giant was a favorite in the betting. A fresh target was set up for him, and all his bullets landed in the black, closely grouped. When Flowers had finished, Tazewell scooping up several shells from the big man's pet pearl-handled six-gun, a scorer at the butts brought his target to the judges.

"Ninety-four!" Dog Wilson bawled the score.

Applause rose at Flowers' fine shooting. He had topped all competitors by several points. He grinned with pleasure, basking in his glory. Jim Hatfield quickly slid past the horses and ducked under the ropes, pushing through the crowd.

"I'd like to try my luck," the Ranger drawled.

"Okay," Dog Wilson replied, with a glance at the tall figure. "Five dollars entry fee."

Hatfield was aware of the startled glances exchanged between Mustang Flowers and Frank Ulman. John Farnsworth was present, though he had taken no part in the match. Men in snakeskin hats edged forward.

But, as the Ranger had figured, Flowers did not dare start anything too crude before the citizens. He must retain his good repute among them.

The atmosphere was tense as the Lone

Wolf stepped up to the stand to fire. Virgil Tazewell, pockets bulging, stood near at hand.

A silence fell as Hatfield delivered his first five shots, almost careless in the speed with which he sent the slugs into the target. He reloaded. From the corner of his eye he saw the sallow Frank Ulman sidle to the judges' table, whisper in Dog Wilson's ear. Hatfield resumed, the steady bang of the big pistol reverberating through the open spaces, explosions almost joined. The Ranger finished, stepped back.

The score came up: "Ninety-seven!"

A gasp rose, then a loud cheer for the big jigger who had bested Flowers. Such shooting was rarely seen.

"Hey, you!" Jim Hatfield swung to look into Sheriff Wilson's earnest, mustached face. "Yuh're under arrest!"

"For what, Dog?" cried Tazewell.

"Settin' fire last night to Ulman's warehouse. Unbuckle yore gunbelt and let her drop."

"I saw him last night, Sheriff!" Blustering, Ulman pushed in. "He tried to murder me. I'll press charges myself."

Ulman's face was dotted with red sears, where that hot lantern glass had struck. A murmur passed through the crowd as its mood changed. "Why, the polecat might've burnt down the whole town!" Flowers said indignantly.

Yet no one seemed to wish to make the first move. The Ranger said easily, "I'll go with yuh, Sheriff."

"Drop yore belt."

Hatfield's eyes coolly surveyed the faces of his enemies. "I'll keep the guns," he drawled.

Dog Wilson cleared his throat, under Hatfield's direct look. "Okay. C'mon."

Tazewell walked at Hatfield's left, the sheriff at the right. The jail was at the edge of the plaza. Citizens strung out behind, and some of Mustang's cohorts began to mention lynching.

Wilson unlocked the door of the brick building which was his office and the town hoosegow. There were two rooms up front, four cells at the rear, cut off from the offices by perpendicular bars set into cement flooring.

The heavy sheriff escorted his prisoner in; Tazewell slipped through the door. Wilson turned on the crowd and shouted at them to disperse. Mustang and his hombres were busy sliding through the gathering, whispering the lynch talk. Wilson swore as he slammed the thick door and shot the bolts.

Hatfield rolled a cigarette.

"Mebbe yuh'll hand over yore guns now, mister," suggested Wilson. "I'll hafta lock yuh up."

The Ranger swung on Tazewell. "Let's see those cartridge cases yuh picked up, Virg."

"Good!" cried Tazewell. "Wilson's okay, Jim." He began to remove small envelopes from his pockets, pencil notations scrawled on each. Wilson's bulldog jaw dropped as he stared at the shining brass shells in their bags.

"Sheriff, these're from the shootin' bee," Hatfield explained. "We got it up for a good reason." He examined the shells carefully, taking his time, pushing one after another into the discard. At last he found what he was hunting; from his pocket he extracted a single shell to compare with those under his hand.

"This is it," he declared.

"Now what's it all about?" asked Wilson.

"Take a look at these, Sheriff, see how they check up with the one I had in my pocket.

Wilson squinted at the brass cylinders; the marks left by the firing-pin were easily seen. "Look the same to me."

"They are. The gun that shot these shells at the match is a well-broken-in weapon, a bit off center with a scarred firin'-pin. This shell I had on me come from the room at Bell ranch where David Horton was murdered."

"Dang my hide! So that's the game!"

Tazewell was excited, too. "Here's the bag the shells were in, Jim."

Eagerly the three stared at the notation. "Marley Bell," the Ranger said, looking at the envelope.

"I'd never've b'lieved it!" exclaimed Tazewell.

"Why, I would," Wilson said, puzzled. "I figgered Bell done it, but never had enough evidence to make the arrest. This sorta cinches it."

Hatfield was silent. Bell was a smart liar. At last the Ranger ordered, "Tazewell, go see if Bell's still in town. If he is, bring him over here."

The lean trapper nodded, slipped from the jail. "Now," Dog Wilson said, "who the hell are yuh, mister?"

The Ranger reached in his inside pocket, drew forth the silver star set on its silver circle, emblem of his famous band.

"A Ranger!" cried Wilson joyfully. "I'm shore glad yuh're here!" He stepped over to his desk, opened a drawer. "I got a lotta things stumpin' me. Here's one: I found this paper under the corpse of Charlie Long, a line rider. Mebbe yuh kin guess what it means. That's only one of the killin's on my hands."

Hatfield stared at the brown paper. There was a dark stain on it. "That's blood," Wilson told him. The paper was thick, with several distinct creases in it.

"Looks as though it'd been round a box," the Ranger said.

"But what're them little black lines?"

"Cancellation lines! This package came by mail."

"Yuh're right! The address was tore off."

Closely Hatfield scrutinized the brown sheet. There were a few small white specks stuck to it. "That's arsenic! This paper's off a package the pizen used across the range come in."

He began to shape the paper into its original creases. With a piece of cardboard Wilson had in his desk, Hatfield quickly formed a dummy package. "Take this over to the post office," he ordered. "The way that arsenic was spread, Wilson, a good many pounds of it was used. Ask the postmaster if he reckernizes this packet; mebbe he'll recall who picked that pizen up."

The crowd outside was still gathered around. Hatfield hitched up his belt, stood

122

smoking, looking out the window. He saw Tazewell coming back, without Marley Bell.

The sky was darkening, with wind clouds that picked up dust and flung it into the faces of the citizens. Men began to head for the saloons.

"Bell's rode out of town," reported Tazewell. "They say the sheepmen were seen west of here today, and on his way to the match some of 'em took a shot at Bell, wounded his horse and one of his riders."

Hatfield's face darkened at this news. Horton, too, had failed him. He knew that he must quickly marshal forces to fight the tremendous forces of evil in the Panhandle, but he must have honest, courageous men —

Wilson came hurrying back. The sheriff cried breathlessly, "The postmaster reckernized that package, Ranger. He says a hull flock of 'em come for One-Eyed Charles Golon. I know Golon; he lives in that square brown place right acrost the plaza, yuh kin see it from this winder. Yuh want me to arrest him?"

A sharp rap on the outer door sent Hatfield back to a cell; he stood, watching as the sheriff looked out. A young man in a white apron shoved a basket in.

123

"From the Okay Restaurant, Sheriff. Supper."

Wilson took the hamper, set it on the desk. He lifted the cover, sniffing hungrily. "Draw up, gents. I'm starved and I'm goin' to it."

Hatfield, pulling together the broken threads of his tentative plans, slowly rolled a cigarette, drew deeply on it as he mulled over the new developments. "Shore tastes good," Wilson said. "Better have some, gents, 'fore I eat it all."

"You're makin' me hungry," said Tazewell, going over.

Hatfield joined them. "Hafta force this Golon to talk," he mused to himself.

The lean trapper held a sandwich and a bottle. "Got a corkscrew?" he asked.

Wilson cleared his throat. He stopped chewing, shifted uncomfortably. He shook his head as though trying to clear his vision.

"Ugh," he grunted thickly. "Boys, I must've eat too fast. Feel sorta funny —" He stood up, hand on the desk.

Hatfield, staring at Wilson with contracted brows, suddenly swept the food from Tazewell's hands. The sheriff staggered, sat down heavily, mouth opening and shutting like a fish out of water. His head banged on the floor and he began twitching spasmodically, the color draining from his face. His lips were gray and his breath came in painful gasps.

"Hustle and fetch a doctor, Tazewell," snapped the Ranger. "He's pizened. Reckon Golon sent me a present in that grub!"

With a curse the startled trapper bounded to the door, ran out, and as the portal opened Hatfield glimpsed the wind-swept plaza, hazy with dust. Violent contortions seized Wilson; his arms stretched, entire body rigid as an iron rod, bowed with weight on head and heels.

"Strychnine," muttered the Ranger, squatted by the sheriff, rendering what first-aid he could. A chilly draught from the banging door sent Wilson into another paroxysm. "Nuthin' to do," Hatfield said. Tazewell should be back with the doctor in a minute.

Cold sweat stood on his forehead. He felt the invisible hand of his foe, checkmating every move he made. The sheriff had seemed an honest, promising ally — but so had Bell and Horton.

Wilson suddenly relaxed. Hatfield felt his pulse. "Dead!" he exclaimed. "No use me stayin' here any longer."

The air of the little jail stifled him and he felt he had to get outside. He rose, and went up front. Honest men had been chased

125

indoors by the storm that had broken over the town. As Hatfield pulled back the door, figures dim in the haze, standing some distance off, set up a howl, bullets clipping the wood frame, nipping at his flesh as he jumped back to cover.

"Escape! Eacape!" an hombre screamed.

Wilson's keys were on the desk, there was a small steel portal at the rear. Gun in hand, he started out, keeping along a fence —

A terrific explosion knocked him flat on his face, rolled him along the grassy earth. Before his sered vision the whole jail rose in an insane, red-yellow sheet of flame, blown to atoms.

He crawled off, deafened as his ears shrieked, debris falling like hailstones. Pulling himself erect he staggered across Main, stood against a side wall. Head down, he recovered from the shock. Men were running toward the blackened hole in the plaza.

One-Eyed Golon's square brown house, pointed out by the dead sheriff, stood nearby. Rage tensed the Ranger's powerful body. He swung to the lane, reached the rear of Golon's. Under his hand a window rose and he climbed in, found himself in a semi-dark bedroom.

Tiptoeing to the door, across a hall he saw a larger chamber; around a table, with a lamp burning in the storm gloom, wind howling outside, four men were sitting. Three wore snakeskin bands on their hats. The fourth was Frank Ulman, the sallow-faced hide dealer, teeth visible as he grinned with satisfaction.

"That spy's done now," chortled Ulman. "The arresting trick worked slick, gents. Dynamite's better than poison."

"Can Mustang and Golon make the B-in-a-Bell in this storm?" a Snake Hat queried.

"Shore. The wind's easing now. They'll fix that Bell girl the way we did the Ranger."

"Guess it got him."

"I'll give a hundred dollars to anyone who can find a chunk bigger than a two-bit piece!" Ulman rose. "Going out to see how it looks." He pushed back his chair.

As Ulman came from the big room he saw Hatfield standing in the opposite doorway. His eyes widened, and his chin dropped.

"You!" hc gasped, "How —" And then the sallow man lost his head, flashed a thin hand for a gun. It had not cleared leather when Hatfield's Colt spat flame a yard from Ulman's middle vest button. The hide dealer folded up like a jack-knife, sliding the wall to the floor. Shouts rose as his pals leaped up at the sound of the shot. Heavy, running steps told the Ranger there were many more inside. He faded back through the bedroom and out the window.

Making was untenable, hundreds of guns hunting him. And he must ride to the B-in-a-Bell, where Mustang and Golon had headed.

Hatfield found Goldy huddled in the shelter of a wall. He nuzzled his master's hand in welcome. The tall jigger threw a leg over the saddle. Goldy went north, the dust storm stinging their faces like needles. Once Hatfield looked around.

"I'll be back!" the Lone Wolf said between clenched teeth.

CHAPTER VIII
HORROR

The dust storm that swept the great plains forced Phil Horton to stop till it began to subside. He was heading for the B-in-a-Bell. He had hoped for word from Lydie but it had not come. Forced back across Rabbit Ear Canyon, refusing to let his men return the fire of pursuing ranchers, he had stayed in the bush and rocks till they had tired of hunting and ridden off. Now, his followers in a hidden camp, he was going alone to see Lydie.

At dark the norther died off and he resumed his journey. His stalwart figure was coated with gray dust when he saw the lights of the Bell ranch. He left his horse in a mesquite thicket and started in afoot. Coming up from the rear, he paused behind a stone springhouse near the kitchen. After a time Lydie opened the door and walked toward him, carrying a pitcher and a platter of food to be placed in the cool springhouse.

Her lovely face was dejected.

"Lydie!" Phil hailed her, stepping out.

Her amber eyes widened. "Phil!" she said then reproachfully, "Why did you do it?"

He misunderstood. "I had to see you," he said eagerly.

"No, I mean why did you let your men make that cowardly attack this morning on father and his men? I had just managed to coax him into good humor and promise to see you."

"Attack — this mornin'?"

There was such honest bewilderment in his voice she stared into his eyes as though trying to read the full truth there. He was close to her, took her hand.

"You know what I mean," Lydie told him. "You sent a request for a truce and then ambushed Dad and his men on their way to Making!"

The charge was so absurd Horton laughed. "That's not true, Lydie. My men were with me all day, in the hills."

She shook her head. "But they recognized Jeff, one of your men. Who else could want to kill father?"

Neither Horton nor Lydie could imagine the gigantic forces of evil that were sweeping them to destruction. She looked up into his handsome face, the breeze stirring the tendrils of her coppery hair. Horton could not resist her beauty and he seized her in his arms, crushed her to him, kissing her yielding lips.

"Lydie, I love you, no matter what!"

She clung to him, "I love you, Phil. I wish — I wish we could settle this war. It makes me afraid, dear."

The night wind moaned in the cotton-woods. Dry leaves rustled and a coyote mourned over the tortured land.

"Father's ridden out with most of our hands, Phil," Lydie said. "But wait, he should soon be home. I'll talk to him and we'll see if we can't make peace."

A woman called from the kitchen, "Lydie, dear, are you all right?"

"Coming, mother," the girl replied. She patted Horton's big hand. "I'll have to go in. But stay here, won't you? I'll come out again as soon as I can."

She stood on tiptoe, to kiss his lips, and, placing the food in the springhouse, went back to the kitchen. Horton found a place of ease along a split-rail fence that formed an outer corral. He closed his eyes, dream-ing of Lydie. Everything else was colored by his love for the young woman.

The sky had cleared and the moon was rising, casting a yellow glow over the prairie.

A crackling noise on the other side of the corral brought Horton up, alert. It might be Marley Bell returning — he looked around. Against the lighter sky, Horton saw a horseman, staring toward the ranch. Beyond him was another, and then still more. A wide ring of them circled their horses but their faces were only black blurs.

He froze as he was. Then sound from the kitchen entry sent his glance that way. Light came from the window at the back, and Horton saw the tall, thin man approaching the door.

"Jeff!" he gasped. His old friend, Jeff Smith, had disobeyed his command, trailed after him.

Horton started to crawl in. He wanted to warn Jeff away, for the silent, menacing horsemen might be cattlemen who would kill him on sight.

The kitchen door opened, and Lydie Bell showed in the opening. Horton heard the man's gruff tones, then Lydie's reply.

"He was here," she told Jeff, "he's waiting for my father, Jeff."

Now Horton saw sinister figures creeping up in back of the bony man facing Lydie Bell. One was a tiny man, a patch over one eye.

"Who's that," Lydie cried suddenly, "right

behind you, Jeff?"

The tall, thin Jeff howled, "This is from the sheepmen! We'll teach yore lousy paw and you a lesson you won't forget!"

Horton leaped up, dashed for the house. In the light from the open doorway showed the pasty, twitching face of the tiny hombre with Jeff. He had an arm raised, and the rays scintillated on a small glass vial gripped in his bony hand.

Phil Horton ripped out his revolver, fired a swift shot as the attacker slid at Lydie. The small man gave a shriek of pain, dancing aside. Jeff reached out, grabbed Lydie Bell before she could jump back inside. The girl began to shout for help, and the line of masked gunmen closed in, whooping, "Sheepmen — this way!"

Horton knew, save for Jeff, they were not his followers. Jeff yelled, voice distorted by fury, "Here she is, Golon, give it to her!" and flung Lydie from the door.

Then Phil was in, and a sudden blast of gun-fire smashed the outer darkness. "Are you crazy, Jeff?" shouted Phil, hotly seizing the old herder's arm, yanking him violently around.

The small man was coming back. Bullets were tearing through the night, men screaming in fury. A huge hombre on a black stallion charged along the line of masked men, on whose Stetsons showed rattlesnake bands. "What's wrong — what's wrong!" the giant bellowed.

That, Phil realized, was Mustang Flowers. Horton turned away from Jeff after yanking him from Lydie; he was staggered, stunned by a hard crack from a pistol barrel that drove him against the house.

"Look out, Phil," Lydie cried, "he's going to shoot!"

Horton swung. The bony Jeff was raising the gun, but Phil Horton could not believe his old retainer would kill him. He put up a hand and from the corner of his eye saw that the small hombre was slipping around him to get at Lydie Bell again.

A hundred mounted men closed in a compact ring about the house. Deadly in aspect, bandannas up, slugs from their flaring guns rattled a death song as Phil Horton confronted Jeff and Golon, the poisoner. A hoarse shout of defiance welled in the young sheepman's throat.

In a moment he would be overwhelmed but he would fight to the end, heart strong.

Then the arc of gunmen on the south side buckled. Horses curveted as their riders yanked furiously at cutting bits. A stentorian war-cry drew their attention for the moment from Horton; Jeff and Golon hesitated, looked around. From behind a barn, with the furious charge of a lightning bolt, two pistols roaring, tearing the masked killers, charged a tall man on a golden sorrel. Men crashed from their saddles; others screeched in agony at wounds from the accurately placed slugs. Startled, snorting mustangs knocked one another, confusing the whole line.

Through the hole he had blasted Jim Hatfield burst at full-speed, the handsome Goldy with teeth nipping, hoofs lashing out, smashing clear.

Mustang Flowers, cursing in frenzy, started at him, bellowing enraged commands. The surprise attack had accomplished its purpose; Hatfield was through, upon the little group outside the kitchen.

"Jim!" cried Horton, recognizing the blood-streaked face of the Ranger. A bullet had furrowed along his scalp, knocked his Stetson off so it hung down his back by its cord.

Even as Hatfield flung himself from the saddle, his Colt spat. Jeff Smith, face twisted with rage, had his revolver against Horton. The lanky sheepman took the bullet from the Ranger's Colt between the shoulder blades; his arms flew out as he flexed, head snapping back in death agony. Horton felt Jeff Smith's lead tear the flesh over his ribs as the bony sheepherder crashed at his feet.

So fast was the action that it was finished in second-fractions. Golon, with a ferocious snarl, sprang at Lydie Bell again, glass vial raised to her face. Horton threw himself between the girl and her attacker, as Hatfield kicked at Golon's body to drive him back. The Ranger, having given Goldy a slap that sent the sorrel running, was in; the poisoner swung on him with a snarl, to dash the viscous white acid at him.

Horton's Colt roared, pointblank in Golon's twisted face. Golon's head went limp on the pipe-stem neck, features melting to a ghastly mask of blood and lacerated flesh, ripped to pulp by the heavy .45 bullet that angled up and lodged in his evil brain.

"Let 'em have it!" The roar of the giant leader rang above the din.

With Golon and Jeff down, the attackers evidently had no longer any reason to hold off firing into the group. Phil Horton felt himself knocked off his feet, as Jim Hatfield scooped Lydie Bell up in one arm and struck the young sheepman with his chest, shoving Horton through the kitchen door. Shielded by the Ranger's body, Lydie fell against the entry wall, out of danger.

The marauders, rallying under the cursing fury of Mustang Flowers, turned their guns on the door. A slug ripped a chunk from Hatfield's disappearing boot, splinters flying thick from the wood as dozens of bullets concentrated on the point where the trio had stood an instant before.

Hatfield turned to slam the thick oak door, and drop the bar in place. Lead thudded into the panels but those bullets that came through were spent. Hatfiefd, grim face streaked with blood from gashed scalp and a nicked cheek, bounded to the table to put out the kitchen lamp.

"Lydie, Lydie! What's wrong?" A comely woman of middle age hurried into the kitchen, round face pale with fright.

"Mother," cried Lydie, as they were plunged into deepening darkness.

"Get inside," Hatfield ordered. "Keep away from them windows."

The attackers had dismounted, and were beginning to shoot through the windows.

Glass crashed, reports ringing in the room.

Horton's brain hummed with horror; Jeff Smith had turned on him, was dead.

He caught his tall friend's orders, "Horton, take 'em in the hall. It's got no windows."

Yells and shots sounded, from the B-in-a-

137

Bell bunkhouse. The Bell retainers, aroused by the melee, had run out into a devastating fire that mowed them down.

At the house itself were only Hatfield and Phil, to protect the women from the furious killers, who were swarming in. In the dim light that filtered from the front room, Horton heard Lydie gasp, "Phil!" Her soft body pressed, trembling with alarm, against him. He put his arm about her protectingly. True courage beat in Horton's steady heart.

The masked murderers were now stamping on the porch, pushing their way in. Others were breaking the window glass in the kitchen to climb through.

The plight of the defenders of the ranch house was serious indeed. But the thought of surrender never suggested itself.

CHAPTER IX
THE POWER OF EVIL

Jim Hatfield, riding fast for the B-in-a-Ball after his narrow escape in Making, had run into the circle of deadly gunmen. Goldy had warned him by uneasy sniffs, telling his master strange horses were close at hand.

A mounted figure against the sky, then another. Stealthily circling, Hatfield had looked in and from a bush screen had seen the horde of masked riders.

With deep, icy courage he had charged through, to rescue Lydie from Golon. His swift instinct had saved Horton from death, Lydie from horrible disfigurement which would forever have scarred her lovely face, blinded those amber eyes.

Drops of the sticky, searing liquid smoked on Hatfield skin; tanned as his hide was, the unpleasant burning kept him rubbing the spots. In his nostrils was the sulphury odor of the concentrated acid.

In the hall, Hatfield realized their position

was unbearable, and his low, precise voice addressed Lydie: "Was that a saddle loft I saw over the kitchen, ma'am?"

"Yes. There's just a ladder up to it."

Gunmen, whooping it up, were thick up front, swinging toward the hall. Others were coming through the window into the kitchen; it was only a matter of seconds before they would be caught between two fires, with no way out.

"Soon as I open fire," Hatfield told Lydie, "scamper acrost and up that ladder — hustle. You too, Horton."

To draw the enemy's attention, the Lone Wolf opened up on the windows as the three he sought to save dashed from the hall for the loft ladder. He could see the dark figures against the opening, and they were bunching, making ready to charge him, as his rapping bullets tore into them. Yelps of pain rang out; some tried to get back through the sash, others returned his fire.

But more were coming at him through the long corridor. Hatfield turned, the booming blast of his Colts throwing panic into the hearts of the assassins. His guns were hot to the touch of his long fingers; he took advantage of the momentary confusion he had caused to scurry left, a hand feeling for the ladder.

"Jim, this way!" Horton's low voice guided him, and the young sheepman's strong hand gripped his wrist. The Ranger started up the ladder, Horton above him. "Get 'em — go get 'em," Mustang Flowers snarled, "they all got to die, boys."

The saddle loft was a low shelf, built under the kitchen eaves. A heavy crossbeam held smaller struts on which rested loose boards. It was crammed with equipment, leather, saddles and harness parts, blankets; from the rafters hung smoked hams and herbs, other meats for the ranch larder.

Back against the wall, saddles nested in front for protection, Lydie and Mrs. Bell crouched. Phil Horton was down low, close to Hatfield, who lay near the edge where he could watch the opposite windows. Guns reloaded, he awaited Mustang's next move.

Men with masked faces, but marked by the snakeband hats, burst from the hall into the kitchen; rattled hombres at the windows fired into their friends before the error was discovered, Flowers cursing frantically.

"They're hid in here somewheres," the giant bawled.

One of them struck a match. In the brief yellow flare killer eyes stared suspiciously about. Heavy boots thudded, as the murderers looked behind the iron cookstove and in the pantries.

"If only father and his men were here!" Hatfield heard Lydie whisper. The match flickered out.

"Light that lamp," snapped Mustang.

Another match flared. Hatfield watched the hombre who had struck it lean over the table to touch it to the wick.

The kitchen was crammed with his enemies. The vermilion circles on the hatbands marked them for the Ranger. The lamp burned up full, but it was several seconds before Mustang Flowers' red-rimmed orbs chanced to rise and catch full the gray-green, cold eyes of Jim Hatfield.

The giant killer froze, mouth dropping open; with a shrill squeak he flashed a huge hand up, pistol rising with it, as he went into action. Mustang dropped behind several of his bunched followers as Hatfield's Colt roared.

Flowers' bullet drilled through the roof over the Ranger. Mustang gave a terrible scream of pain. The men below were thick; Phil Horton began to shoot along with the Ranger, and they could not miss, every slug struck flesh and bone. The killers began to stampede, and bellow like frightened steers, as they fought only to reach the exits. Crowding bodies struck the table, and the lamp toppled, struck the floor with a glassy crash.

Blackness again was over the kitchen. But the oil from the lamp spread across the dry boards. A tiny flicker of flame caught and rose. The kerosene flared up to burn. When the room once more showed distinct, it was empty save for the dead who lay as they had fallen, trampled in the rush. Mustang Flowers was gone.

But there were still men in the hall. Hatfield swung his guns that way, hot lead driving back those who dared to show. He ceased firing for a minute to speak to Horton.

"Pass me some of them blankets, Horton," he ordered. Horse blankets were piled in a corner. Phil brought over an armful, and the Ranger took them, went down the ladder, beat at the oil fire.

The smoke billowed up and the flames singed him; but he smothered the blaze. Horton, from the balcony, covered him, guns holding them away from the kitchen. Hatfield hustled back to the loft.

Outside, the horde of gunmen had rallied, maddened by the stiff resistance of Hatfield and Horton. Brands were lighted, they could see the red flares in the night, through the window openings. The house walls were of thick adobe, that would not ignite, but there was plenty of wood trimming and furnishings that would. In spiteful fury, and to drive the victims out where they could be slaughtered, fires were started up front, and flaming sticks tossed into the kitchen.

Again, as a torch took hold on the oil-soaked kitchen floor, the Ranger had to make his way down to fight it with more blankets. Bullets ripped through the smoke but it was so thick they had difficulty placing him. He looked through the hall; the front room was burning, woodwork and chairs afire. He knocked over a masked hombre who crossed his range of vision, and returned to the loft.

He knew it was only a question of time. Alone he might have run the gauntlet and made it; with the women, one elderly and frightened to hysteria, it could not be accomplished. The whooping of the killers outside was a brutal paean of death. The minutes passed agonizedly.

"I'm stifling," Mrs. Bell choked. Lydie, too, gasped for breath, coughing spasmodically, as the acrid smoke billowed through the hall, rising into the loft.

"We can't stick here much longer," Horton said, a tense note in his voice.

Hatfield rose up. The roof was within

reach and he found an old axe in a corner. With several blows of his powerful arms he beat a hole through. A gush of fresh air struck his face, the draught sucking up the smoke and fire toward them. Hatfield enlarged the opening, hoisted his long body to the flat roof of the hacienda. A two-foot adobe brick parapet ran around the sides. He hailed Horton softly, and Phil boosted up Mrs. Bell, then Lydie, the Ranger lifting the women up beside him.

In the fresher air they quickly recovered from the effects of the smoke. Hatfield, Colts loaded and ready, made a swift survey. The roof was clear of the enemy; he reconnoitered, could see row after row of men, sitting their horses off in the darkness, waiting for their victims to emerge from the fire-gutted house. He could not place Mustang Flowers.

"I hope I didn't kill him," he muttered. "Figger he's been my ace in this game and I can still play him!" For Flowers, directly brutal as he was, had led the Lone Wolf to valuable information. Behind the giant Hatfield knew there was someone much more powerful, whose brain directed the gigantic conspiracy against the State of Texas, someone who had tried to poison him, had planted dynamite beneath the jail floor to blow him to pieces.

He saw through drifting smoke the stone springhouse near the back corner. He formed a tentative plan to lower the women to the ground and make a final dash for it when the flames grew too hot to bear. It would only mean a brief interlude, but the thought of Lydie Bell and her mother falling into those murderous hands was not pleasant to dwell upon.

The flat roof was hot under their bodies as they crouched low to keep from being seen by those below. Smoke forcing up, clogged their lungs, and their eyes stung, watered, in spite of the breeze, blowing off the prairie, that carried some of the vapor away.

The attackers had not yet realized they had escaped from the kitchen. But the red glow was increasing in extent, as the fire billowed up. Hatfield cast a calculating glance toward the rear angle, where a drain pipe might assist in reaching the ground. He came up on his knees, knowing they must try that fatal dash for the stone springhouse.

"Callate we better be movin'," he said softly.

The grim-faced Horton had a protecting arm around Lydie's slim shoulders. He nodded; the bravery of the young man, Hatfield thought, was a help. No weakening showed in his eyes, red-rimmed from the smoke, from the tense fight and the torturesome waiting for the end. The Ranger crawled along the inner edge of the balustrade, leading the way.

"I'll go down first," he told Phil Horton. "Yuh lower Mrs. Bell and Lydie and I'll catch 'em."

As the tall jigger rose above the level of the rail, masked men, snake hats visible, sighted him through the drifting smoke. Yells of hatred rang out, and they began to fire at him as he rapidly opened upon them with his Colt to blast a few seconds respite for the women.

CHAPTER X
GUNS OF HATRED

Hatfield swung a long leg over the railing. The searing rip of a bullet touched his cheek, and his pistol blazed an answer to the guns of hate.

Then shots sounded from the west. As the enemy rushed up to concentrate on him, kill him before he could drop to the ground, heavy shouting told the Ranger that help was coming. A cowboy whoop rang from the dark-shadowed prairie.

"That's Dad!" gasped Lydie. "Thank God he's come."

Hatfield slid back onto the roof, hurried to the front, across the hot roof. Rallied by their lieutenants, the masked hombres were lining up to meet the incoming cowmen, at the head of whom rode the wiry Marley Bell.

The Ranger leaped to the parapet, outlined in the fiery glow. "Bell this way! Watch yore hides!"

Cursing men swung to finish him, but his Colts opened on them, ripping their line, throwing confusion into the long ranks. Marley Bell, with forty riders strung out in uneven formation, jumped to the conclusion the sheepmen had attacked his home; in fury the two lines met, the clash audible over the roar. Pistols blazed pointblank as cursing hombres maneuvered for position; the cowboys rode with the pell-mell, careless ease of men born to the saddle, and the raiders were framed against the blazing house.

Jim Hatfield's deadly shooting in the rear stung them to madness. The Ranger could not see Mustang Flowers among the attackers, evidently the giant had fled after the Ranger had wounded him. The Lone Wolf jumped to the lower roof of the front veranda, and, hanging at the side, let himself drop to the ground.

He came up with both pistols barking. Bullets whirled thick, whistling in air, thudding into flesh and bone. The din was tremendous, confusion prevailing as the battle raged. Hatfield, on one knee, squeezed against the porch corner, picked off two bosses of the snakeband raiders. Horses reared, jerking at their bits; the B-in-a-Bell, Marley in the thick of it, fought with a vicious courage that finally overcame the greater numbers of the enemy. The enfilading fire of the Ranger completed the rout, panicking the hearts of the hired gunmen. Without Mustang Flowers to lead them, and appalled by the terrific fighting ability of Jim Hatfield, the shaken marauders gave up.

Men swung their foam-flecked mustangs to get out of that light area where they were being picked off one after the other; the screams of wounded was not enheartening. Then groups followed suit, till the entire gang of killers was in wild flight, galloping south across the shadowed plains toward Making City.

The cursing, hot-tempered Marley Bell, reloading his guns, ordered his men to pursue. Faster and faster the horsemen flew through the night; here and there a cowboy caught up with a gunman and there was a swift exchange of bullets, after which only one figure rode away from the spot.

As the shooting grew less, the split marauders riding in all directions to escape the infuriated B-in-a-Bell contingent, Jim Hatfield rose up, gave several shrill whistles. He started to the rear of the house, calling to Horton, who was guarding the two women, still on the roof. Horton first lowered Mrs.

Bell over the railing, then Lydie. The Ranger caught them and set them safely on the ground.

Hatfield swung around as the giant golden sorrel galloped up to him, nuzzled his long hand, stained with powder.

Marley Bell, anxious as to the fate of his wife and daughter, came whirling back with most of his men, having chased the gunmen far out into the night. He threw himself from his saddle, started inside the burning house. Mrs. Bell screamed to him, and he turned, running toward them, face black with smoke, eyes glowing, a streak of blood across his cheek where a bullet had clipped him. His nostrils flared wide, breath coming in great heaves from exertion.

"Mary — Lydie — yuh all right?" he gasped.

"Yes, yes, Marley." His wife threw herself into his arms.

Suddenly Bell recognized Phil Horton, standing with an arm around Lydie. Then he saw the tall, quiet Hatfield, a hand on the golden sorrel's arched neck. With a roar of rage, Bell leaped at Horton's throat, hand starting for his holstered six-gun. Lydie tried to step between the two men but her father thrust her aside.

"Damn yuh, Horton! This is yore doin'.

151

I'll kill yuh for it —"

Hatfield seized the angry man, pulled him away from Horton, who would not strike Lydie's father. Hotly Bell bawled for his men.

"Boil down, Bell," the Ranger drawled.

"Father, Phil and Jim saved our lives!" cried Lydie.

"That's the truth, Marley," corroborated Mrs. Bell. "A gang of awful masked sheepmen attacked us."

"That's what I'm sayin'. Hell's bells, Horton's gang done this!"

"That bunch of devils wasn't mine," growled Phil, "except for Jeff Smith. He must have gone loco to travel with those murderers; he'd dead now."

Marley, rage against Horton cooling off a little because of his wife's and Lydie's words, raised a hand to restrain men, who were running to him.

"Bell, yuh better get busy dousin' that fire," Hatfield advised. "It's guttin' yore house. We'll chew this all over when it's out."

Marley swung, snapping orders to his followers, and the efficient frontiersmen hurriedly formed bucket lines to the pond, set to work extinguishing the blaze.

Hatfield and Phil started to help. A hoarse

call reached them from the dense shadows behind the springhouse. "Phil, you danged fool," the voice called, "run for it!"

Horton's mouth dropped open in stunned amazement. "Why, that was Jeff Smith's voice," he said, gripping the Ranger's wrist. "I'd 've sworn it, Jim — !"

Hatfield started for the springhouse. And Jeff Smith, buffalo gun in his hands, skeleton face grim, rose up from the dark patch; Olly Crouse was right with him.

"C'mon, c'mon," Jeff Smith told Horton anxiously. "Them cowmen 'll string you up, Phil. Are you loco, standin' around this way? The boys're here. We heard the shootin', seen the fire glow and rode to bring you off."

"Jeff, I thought you were dead, I don't savvy it," Phil Horton exclaimed.

Jim Hatfield turned and hurried to the kitchen. Right outside lay the long, death-struck figure of that lanky dark-clad hombre they had thought was Jeff Smith. Go-lon, smashed head a horrible sight, sprawled close at hand. The Ranger stooped to make a swift examination. His face was bleak when he rose. "Rigged up as a spittin' image of that bony sheepman," he muttered, "to make Bell shore it was they who throwed that acid! No doubt about it," he added, "that sidewinder's a master at disguisin'."

Over at the bunkhouse, he found a dozen slaughtered Bell punchers, mowed down when they ran out in answer to the cries of distress from Lydie and her mother. Fury burned in the tall jigger's breast, an answering hatred for the ruthless foe he sought to exterminate, the man who had sent Golon to throw vitriol into the lovely face of Lydie Bell and who had brought ruin and death to Northwestern Texas.

The Ranger swung back to Horton. "Keep yore men away from these cowboys till we clear this up, Phil," he ordered. "We don't want any more feudin'. I'll talk to Marley Bell soon as I can."

The fire was under control. The brick walls did not crumble and with buckets of water and heavy blankets, the cowmen extinguished the flames. Marley Bell stepped back, took off his Stetson to wipe pouring sweat from his blackened, bloodstained face. Jim Hatfield touched his arm.

"Bell, I rode out here to talk with yuh. I run into that gang of killers. Now I reckon the time has come for us to parley."

"What yuh want of me?" demanded Bell truculently. "I thought the sheriff had yuh in Making jail. Yuh snatched Horton from me — though what yuh done tonight makes

154

up for a lot."

Hatfield's jaw was set. He drew out the telltale shells he had collected from the shooting bee, and the particular one Lydie had found in the room where David Horton died.

"When yuh claimed yuh hadn't killed Dave Horton I b'lieved yuh. But here's the evidence. That contest was to check the guns in the community."

"What the hell yuh drivin' at?" muttered Bell.

"Jest this: the shells from yore Colt match the one that finished Dave Horton. Yuh could've ejected an empty cartridge and reloaded after yuh shot him."

"Why, damn yuh —" snarled Bell.

Hatfield had his wrist in an iron grip. "Yuh know guns, Bell, so do I. The one in yore holster right now is the pistol yuh used at the match. Let's have it."

"Go ahead, take it."

The Ranger drew the smooth-stocked .45. It had a beautiful balance, and was well broken in. He pointed it into the air, pulled the hammer back and let go. Breaking it, he extracted the fired shell, held it to a lighted lantern.

"Well?" Bell growled.

The markings on the murder cartridge

and the one beside it, in the Ranger's calloused palm, matched exactly. "Tazewell wouldn't make any mistake, markin' sech," remarked Hatfield coldly. His gray-green eyes drilled Marley Bell, who lost his aplomb, grew rattled.

"Listen, mister, yuh gotta believe me," cried Marley. "I kin prove by witnesses that my pet gun was stole from the rack in Making restaurant. Then Frank Ulman, the hide dealer, offered to sell me this one cheap. It's a beauty, and I used it in the match. But I never kilt Dave Horton, I've only had the hogleg twenty-four hours." His voice was very earnest. "Ulman must've planted me."

"There's been plenty plantin' in the Panhandle," the Ranger drawled. "While yuh've fought sheepmen and shadders, Bell, control of the country's passed into outlaw hands. Men who laid pizen wholesale through the whole of the Northwest; who fixed up as sheepmen to trick yore friends and smash their power. Who started the Comanches raidin', to spread panic among the citizens."

"But — why — why? What's the sense of it?" cried the bewildered cattle king.

"Callate on havin' it all straight in a day or so. Now yuh make a truce with Phil Horton and save yore lead for the real enemy."

Bell's hot gaze met the full gleam of the tall jigger's; the chief of the cowmen was first to drop his eyes. "I'll do it. Yuh say that pizen wasn't planted by sheepmen. An hour ago I'd have called yuh a liar, but since yuh've showed me how some sidewinder tried to pin that murder on me, I'll take yore word."

"How many fightin' men kin yore association muster if need be?"

"Oh, a couple hunderd. Why?"

"I'll need them and plenty more. We're facin' a small army. Hell's due to bust loose any minute. Send word to yore friends to quit huntin' sheepmen and collect here."

Hatfield turned away, sang out to Phil Horton, who came to him.

"Bell's ready to call the war off, Horton. Shake hands."

Marley held out his, and the young man took it.

The Ranger called Goldy, swung a leg over the sorrel's saddle. "Where yuh bound, Jim?" Horton asked.

"Making City. I could use yuh. Got somethin' heavy to tote."

Horton's eyes lighted. "Wait'll I get my horse."

"Pick a good one," counseled Hatfield. "And order yore men to camp near here so

157

yuh kin find 'em quick. Tell 'em yuh've made a truce with the cattlemen."

It was still dark when the two stalwart young men reached the outskirts of Making. The Ranger drew up close to a deep gully, fringed by heavy mesquite and chaparral, which ran east and west, splitting the plain.

"They'll be watchin' for me, Phil, and I wanta stay hid. Pull down yore hat and keep to the back lanes, ride in and hire a small, well-covered wagon at the big livery stable this end of town. Hustle back here with it."

Horton nodded, cantered off, disappeared beyond the buildings. Twenty minutes later he returned, driving a small, light wagon with a black-painted wooden top, his own saddle horse tied behind. At the Ranger's command, he led his mustang down a sliding sand path into the hidden gully, and they left Goldy and Horton's animal concealed in the ditch.

Phil Horton took the reins, pushed back against the seat, and Hatfield crouched inside the wagon body. They clattered into Main Street, headed south.

From a peep-hole Hatfield could look out and see the heavily armed gunmen, rattlesnake hatbands showing, who stalked the awninged walks of the big town. Without

158

doubt they were looking for trouble, for him, but he stayed in the confines of the wagon, which did not draw more than a few incurious glances as it slowly proceeded toward the railroad tracks. There were plenty of teams and horses around, despite the hour, and Phil, in his dusty blue suit, felt hat down, looked like a farmer coming to town for a load of supplies.

"What's the game?" he inquired.

"I mean to snaffle Mustang Flowers."

Horton's eyes swept the ominous hombres in the streets. "There he is now!" he exclaimed.

The giant chief of gunmen appeared on the porch of a small house that overlooked the plaza. A fresh white bandage was visible, plastered on his cheek, and he could put hardly any weight on his left leg.

Mustang limped painfully along the walk, and swung toward a square brown house, which Hatfield knew had sheltered the dead poisoner Golon, where the Ranger had shot down Frank Ulman, the hide dealer.

"Callate that's headquarters," drawled Hatfield.

At his order Phil turned the livery stable team off Main. They then swung along the lane behind the Main Street buildings. "Pull up behind this barn," Hatfield said. "We don't wanta get too close or they'll spot us."

They left the wagon, Horton silently treading in his friend's steps, approaching the rear of the brown structure.

That bedroom window was open. Hatfield's duel with Ulman had been so swift, his escape in the darkness of the windstorm so timed, that the men inside the place had failed to identify him, though they might guess he had paid them a visit. Crouched down, the two listened to voices inside.

"Friday's the big day, Mustang," a deep, resonant one was saying. "D' you think you'll be able to lead the men?"

"Shore," Flowers growled. "I'll have eight hundred fighters in Making on Friday. No one kin stop us now. But Jarvis swore he'd take keer of that Ranger jigger. And he didn't 'cause I seen him out at the B-in-a-Bell and I don't doubt it was him who shot Ulman. 'Twas his fault I'm wounded and that we missed out there."

"Never mind. I'll use that fight in my speech, lay it all on the war. One man can't worry us."

"Uh! He kilt Golon, Ulman and a dozen of my pards," snarled Flowers. "But we're too strong for him. Our commissioners 'll whip the Comanches into line agin."

"What do you figure on doing with the

160

Indians, once we've finished the job?"

"That's easy. Throw a few bullets into 'em and chase 'em back acrost the Staked Plain. Yuh didn't think we'd leave 'em have any good range land, did yuh? Jest watch my smoke. The State of Jefferson 'll handle them red devils so fast ev'ry citizen'll be happy to fork out extra taxes.

"Long Lance ain't got more'n five hunderd braves and half of 'em refused to throw in with us. It'll be a cinch — and so'll finishin' Bell and his gang. They're near busted now, and once the guv'nor's in power, which 'll be Friday, we'll condemn their land and chase the whole parcel out. Now beat it, John. I'm plumb wore out and that leg wound stings like fire."

"Okay, Mustang. Friday we split Texas — and to hell with her. I'll make a speech that'll sway the country."

A door banged. Hatfield went over, peered up the alley. Against lighted Main Street he saw a stout, short figure, hurrying away.

"Farnsworth! A pal of Mustang's! And it was Mustang's hombre Blackie who took that shot at him. Huh. Jest a play, to rouse the crowd and get their sympathy!"

CHAPTER XI
HOSTAGE

Hatfield had discovered a great deal at the square house. That Flowers was a powerful henchman, close to the top, in the confidence of the evil brain behind the tremendous events gripping the Panhandle in tense excitement. Who was Jarvis, the governor, who had sworn to finish him? On Friday the Ranger knew he must face hundreds on hundreds of hostile guns.

Even if he mustered the Bell and Horton cohorts, they would be overwhelmed. Provided he got close enough to the vital gathering which would be held in Making Friday. But citizens of the big town would look upon him as an arsonist, probably as a killer, after that explosion at the jail. The tremendous forces of his enemy were marching with devastating speed, and he had only two days left in which to strike them a crippling blow.

Every moment they remained in the lane

added to the danger of discovery. In the slow wagon they could not hope to run for it if their enemies chanced upon them —

The rugged face of the great Ranger was lined with determination. Overwhelmed by the seething masses he fought, where two sprang up for every one he disposed of, he knew he must swiftly reach the governor, the chief of this ruthless organization.

He knew what their game was: to form a new state, voted for by alarmed citizens for protection against the supposed Indian uprising and the seemingly widespread sheep-cattle war, which had paralyzed business, placed the lives of innocents in jeopardy. Such state control would provide the governor with tremendous power and wealth, with his crooked political henchmen. The people, tricked into electing the murderous governor, would be milked dry by taxes; the best land would be seized by condemnation proceedings — all the usual methods of graft.

Mustang Flowers' heavy snoring was audible; the giant gunman was utterly exhausted, and weakened by his wounds.

"Here we go," whispered Hatfield. He pressed lengths of rope into Horton's hands, and pushed the window softly all the way up. He shoved through into the darkened bedroom, and could make out Flowers' huge body stretched on the cot.

Phil Horton was at his elbow. "I'll hold him down and keep him from yellin'," Hatfield told the young man. "You tie him up."

They tiptoed across to the bed. Hatfield, working with unerring precision, threw himself upon Mustang, his left hand taking a throat hold tight as the crushing jaws of a steel vise, right jamming a crumpled bandanna into Mustang's big mouth, that stifled all but a muffled grunt of alarm as Flowers awoke. The Ranger's knee drove all the breath from the struggling man's lungs, and a tap from a Colt butt stopped all resistance.

Hurriedly they tied his wrists behind him, secured the gag, toted the heavy gunman to the window. The way was clear and, running their captive to the barn between them, they rolled him into the wagon, threw a blanket over his limp form, and started out of Making by way of the rear lanes.

Red streamers of dawn showed in the sky behind them as, having reached their hidden horses, they lowered the wagon down the slide into the gully. Mustang was transferred to the back of the livery stable horse, and then they headed across the prairie.

Horton heaved a deep sigh. "That was

'bout as neat a play as I ever saw," he cried. "Let's take him out to my camp, Jim. We can work on him there, and it's not far."

The Ranger shook his head, eyes on the lightening sky. "I got a long ride ahead, Phil. Figger on killin' two birds with one stone. I'm goin' all the way to them hills north of the Staked Plain."

"But the Comanches are there!"

Hatfield nodded. "That's why I'm takin' Flowers there. Yuh ride on to the B-in-a-Bell and make certain Marley has his friends together, by dawn Friday. See they're well-armed, and yore own men too. Yuh'll hear from me. I'm stakin' all I got on this play with Flowers."

"You'll be back Friday morning?"

The tall jigger nodded. "Mebbe Thursday night. If not by then — never."

"S'pose something breaks while yuh're away?"

"Get in touch with Virgil Tazewell, the trapper, in Making. He's a friend of mine and he'll do ev'rything he kin to help. I'd 've connected with him last night, but they're watchin' him and his place for me and I couldn't take any chances of ruinin' our game. *Adios*."

Phil Horton sat his saddle, watching the Ranger trot off westward, leading the horse

165

with Mustang Flowers tied across its back, looking like a bulky sack of meal under a blanket.

When Hatfield had dropped from sight beneath the rolling plain, Phil turned and spurred back toward the Bell ranch. Tired from his long run without sleep, Horton made as fast time as he could.

Marley Bell was still up, and Phil delivered Hatfield's message. Riders had been dispatched to call in members of the Panhandle Grazers, with their armed followers.

Lydie fixed some breakfast for Phil, in the charred kitchen, smelling of the fire. The dead had been picked up and buried, the wounded cared for.

Finishing his meal, Phil kissed the girl's soft lips, and crossed the yard, rounding the pond to the spot where his sheepmen had camped. They greeted him gladly, and he curled up in a blanket to rest.

Many thoughts rushed through his excited mind. The death of his father had been a terrible blow and he knew he would never forget the fine man he had loved, who had brought him up and taught him honesty and industry, and instilled in him the principles of righteousness, bequeathed him a strong body and the bravery of pioneer blood.

But in the Panhandle he had found the

woman he adored. And there was Jim, his new friend; Phil thought he had never met any man who so strongly affected him with a deep admiration and loyalty.

He fell asleep, did not waken till darkness had set in. Jeff Smith and Olly Crouse squatted near at hand, talking in low tones so as not to disturb him. The other sheepmen lounged about, around a small fire.

Horton sat up, yawned and stretched. Jeff grunted, "Hey, Phil! Thought you was gonna sleep forever. We're gittin' purty hungry. S'pose you could dig up some grub at the house?"

Phil nodded and rose, starting for the hacienda on the other side of the pond. He would see Lydie and that raised his youthful spirit. Tomorrow would be Thursday — and after that came the fatal day when Jim would make his final play.

He skirted the pond, reached the kitchen. There was a light inside and Mrs. Bell was busy cooking. She smiled when she saw him in the door, invited him in.

"I suppose Lydie just couldn't tear herself away," she cried.

He was puzzled. "What do you mean, ma'am?"

"Why, she's with you, isn't she? She took a basket of food over to your camp half an

167

hour ago."

Terror streaked through Horton's heart. He licked his lips. "I didn't see her. She hasn't been at our camp."

Mrs. Bell's face grew worried. "That's queer. Wait, maybe she's out at the bunk-house." She stepped to the door and called sharply, "Lydie!"

The only answer was the echo of her voice from the surrounding walls. Horton snatched a lantern and started around the pond. Tracks of men and horses were thick here, close to the home ranch, and it was impossible to pick out an individual trail. He reached his friends, and torches were lit at the fire. They began to cast about in widening circles, and Mrs. Bell joined them.

"There's the basket she was carrying," cried the mother suddenly.

Phil hurried over. The contents had been spilled out. To the handle was pinned a white sheet of paper, and he snatched it, read the rough scrawl:

"Bell, if you come near Making before Saturday you'll never see her again. Otherwise she'll be released without being harmed. Don't try to trail us." There was no signature.

Marley Bell, summoned, read the ominous note from the kidnapers who had slipped in out of the dark like wraiths, seized Lydie and spirited her off. He began to curse madly. His child was the joy of his life.

At his hot commands, every man at the ranch saddled up, and lines of riders swept out, cutting through the moonlight of the bush-shadowed plain, hunting some sign to follow. But the kidnapers had ridden unshod horses, and on the dry earth were myriad tracks, that the wind would soon obliterate.

Horror gripping his heart, Phil Horton rode on, praying he might run upon something to help in the search. If they disobeyed the command in the note, not to come to Making, he did not doubt that the hidden enemy would kill Lydie without the slightest compunction; the attempt to throw vitriol in her eyes to prolong the war between the cowmen and his followers showed how fiendishly brutal that foe was.

He could not remain still. He wished Jim were with him, but by this time the tall jigger would be far to the west, unaware of this horrible development.

Then he remembered Virgil Tazewell. Jim had told him the trapper was a friend, to apply to in case of trouble. But Tazewell was in Making, where the kidnapers had forbidden them to go.

"Have to try it, anyway," he muttered,

wiping the cold sweat off his brow. Tazewell might know what to do.

Yet he dared not rush Making with a large body of fighting men; that might mean Lydie's instant death. Desperate, he decided to sneak in alone, and he stuck spurs into his horse, galloping south at a breakneck pace.

Knowing that Tazewell's warehouse and quarters stood at the south end of town, he rode a wide circle and came up across the tracks. Before him the big town hummed with excitement; he could hear snatches of music from the saloons, and shouts of drunken and merrymaking men. Main Street was filled with horses and wagons, the sidewalks crammed with strolling citizens. Among them strode heavily armed hombres, in Stetsons trimmed by the rattlesnake band with vermilion circle.

Dismounting in the darkness, Phil Horton crept toward Tazewell's, remembering that Hatfield had told him the place was being watched by the enemy. There was a light on the north side.

Horton flitted from shadow to shadow. He reached a rear door, and found that it was unlocked. He pushed inside the main storage chamber, odorous pelts and hides piled about. And across the wide floor he could see the small lighted room where he hoped to find the trapper.

As he started for it a lantern was uncovered, flashed in his eyes. Cocking guns clicked, men leaping upon him.

"Grab him!" a harsh voice snarled.

Phil Horton's hand flew to his gun; a shot roared and he felt the burning bullet sear his right forearm. An instant later a dozen attackers gripped him, pinning his wrists and legs. They threw him down, as he fought them fiercely, kicked him, beat him without mercy. The powerful Horton had a fighting heart, but he could accomplish little against the hands that held him.

Overwhelmed in the rush he was subdued, brain singing from brutal blows, crashing thuds of pistol barrels on head and neck; spurred boots drove into his ribs. Tied hand and foot, dirty paws stifling any outcry, he was bodily dragged across the floor to the light shaft that came from the small room.

Snake Hats were in complete control of Tazewell's. They surrounded him. From the shadows beyond, that ugly voice snapped, "Well, sheepman! Where's your Ranger friend? I hoped that was him we had."

Horton peered into the gloom but all he could make out were glowing eyes over a mask blur. "I came here to see Virgil Tazewell," he growled, no weakness of fear in his voice.

A Snake Hat laughed. "Huh. Tazewell's done for —"

"Tazewell's through," the boss broke in. "He can't help you. We've got him under control and all of Making. Your one chance to live and save your sweetheart is to help me."

The hombres holding Phil Horton swung him so that he looked through into the lighted room.

A gunman stepped over, lifted a blanket draped over someone in the corner. It was Lydie Bell, tied to a chair. Her face was drained of color, her head slumped on her shoulder in a dead faint.

"How would you enjoy seeing that pretty face burned by hot irons, Horton?" inquired the sinister chief, speaking from the darkness outside. "I want to know where your friend is."

Phil braced himself. He could stand anything himself, but if they hurt Lydie — ! Rescue was impossible, he knew that. No one knew where he had come and even if Bell brought his forces to Making, they would be crushed by the great numbers of Snake Hats who had the town in charge.

Another Snake Stetson came into the

warehouse from the street, approached the gathering about Horton. "Hey, Guv'nor Jarvis," he growled, "we ain't been able to trace Mustang or find hide nor hair of him. He's jest dropped outa sight."

The hombre baiting Phil cursed furiously. "The big fool," he snarled. "A hundred to one that cursed Ranger's behind this." Ferociously he swung on Phil. "What d' yuh know of it all, Horton? Come on, talk, and make it fast!"

Horton called forth every reserve of his fortitude. He would not betray his friend; he fought to clear his brain, to discover a way out, for Lydie and himself.

CHAPTER XII
THE PLAY

That night, after riding all day through the dusty heat, pausing only to pour a little water down the throat of the now conscious, rolling-eyed Mustang Flowers, Jim Hatfield looked ahead and saw a faint glow in the sky over the dark foothills. That marked the fires of Chief Long Lance's temporary encampment in the foothills north of the Staked Plain.

Hatfield was staking everything on this play. There would be no time for another, even if he survived. And, should he fail, Northwest Texas was lost, its citizens in the clutches of a venal organization.

The young braves, after Hatfield had killed Pruitt had rejoined the main tribe farther back in the hills. Before reaching the hollow in which was Long Lance's camp, the Ranger pulled off the trail and left Flowers, tied and gagged, behind a rock-pile. He wanted to survey the scene before riding in.

A streamer of moonlight shone on the Ranger's grim face as he made ready to cast the dice in this life-or-death game. He dropped Goldy's reins and crept on foot over rocky slopes, silent as a stalking red-skin, avoiding the Indian sentinels.

Peering down from the ridge shadows he saw the pow-wow going on. Naked braves, bodies glistening in the ruby firelight, faces streaked by vermilion to ferocious masks, gathered about a main blaze, listening to a pair of men wearing the rattlesnake band on their hats. The visitors were exhorting Comanches to continue their raids. The commissioners had brought along two pack-horses laden with trinkets as bribes.

Chief Long Lance sat, majestic figure with back straight as an arrow, on a colored blanket, staring into the tongues of flame. His medicine man, Singing Bear, in eerie cloak of grizzly skin, crouched at his right. The fat commissioner was speaking. "One more big raid," he shouted, in their tongue, "and the Comanches of the Staked Plain will have won back their hunting grounds! I bring you gifts from the great white chief of the new State, Governor Jarvis. He will not allow anyone to punish you for what you do!"

Hatfield started down the slope, a moving

shadow in the darkness. Rapidly he came up to the light circle edge, and raised a hand in token of friendship. Startled black eyes turned upon him, and Comanche braves fingered the rifles hidden under their blankets.

He spoke their tongue, with the stolid but flowery manner of speech which the Indians required. "I have come," he said in Comanche, "to prove to you the Snake Hats are liars! They bring death and ruin to all of you!"

The fat commissioner cursed, face red as a beet. He made a bad error, slapping his hand to his Colt-butt that rode in the holster, bulging out by his stomach. Hatfield's pistol smashed the air of the hollow, report banging from the surrounding tops. The hombre from Making clutched his throat, crashed at his friend's feet.

The second man took one look at the set Ranger, whose blue-steel weapon, with its staring black muzzle, was ominously swinging his way. He turned with a hoarse scream and ran full-tilt away. Chief Long Lance snatched up a Winchester rifle and calmly planted a shot between his shoulder blades.

The savages were on their feet, grabbing their rifles. Fierce, painted faces turned on Hatfield. "He has come again!" cried Singing Bear.

Long Lance was friendly toward Hatfield; he was furious that the Snake Hats had split his authority, bribed his young men away from his control. And the old chief was too experienced not to realize that only evil could come upon his tribe from the raids on Texas.

Hatfield went to Long Lance, spoke in his ear. The chief nodded. They hurried back down the trail, returning with the trussed Mustang Flowers.

"You recognize this man, Comanches," Hatfield told them. "He's a great chief among the Snake Hats and knows all their secrets."

The younger braves grouped themselves apart, listening. They all pressed in as Hatfield dumped Mustang Flowers on the dirt in front of the main fire.

The giant gunman, responsible for so many deaths and intense horror in the Panhandle, faced his own fate with little courage. Already he was miserable from the bonds on his limbs; his wounds ached and he was broken by fear of the tall jigger who had fought back at him and his cohorts with such efficient savagery. Tough as Mustang considered himself, he realized that he bucked up against a man who could give him odds at any fighting game.

"Take off gag," said Long Lance, speaking stilted, broken English so the prisoner would understand his words. "We like hear squeal."

Hatfield ripped off the bandanna. Mustang licked dry lips, drew in a deep breath of the smoky air. "Hey," he growled, "what the hell's the idee, damn yuh!"

"The quicker yuh tell the truth, Mustang, the quicker it'll be over," Hatfield told him coldly. He waved a hand to Long Lance.

The chief's nostrils flared. His face lines were emotionless though in the dark eyes the firelight reflected back with an animal gleam. There was a guttural command and two older braves brought several long steel bars which they thrust into the redhot coals of the fire.

Long Lance drew his hunting knife, its razor-sharp blade scintillating. He stooped and placed the cutting-edge so that it rested by the knife's weight on Flowers' gulping throat. The circle of Indians pressed forward with pleased expectancy.

"Don't — don't!" whispered Mustang, his horsy eyes roving with terror.

Hatfield squatted at Flowers' head. "Tell Long Lance what yuh intend to do to the Comanches, once yuh've split the Panhandle off Texas."

"Why — we mean to give 'em back all the land they lost," quavered Mustang.

Hatfield looked at Long Lance. "I guess we better wait till those bars are hot," he said in English.

Long Lance swung to give an order, and an Indian brought one of the glowing irons, a piece of lashed hide serving as a handle. The big chieftain expertly drew the hot point along the tender nerves over Flowers' high cheek bones, and a scream issued from the tortured man's throat. The odor of singed flesh rose into the air.

Hatfield's countenance was as stolidly emotionless as any Comanche's. The red-hot end of the metal bar had left a brown sear against the lighter yellow of the giant gunman's cheek. Again it descended, very slowly, the point aimed at his right eye, only turning at the last instant to burn the flesh over the other cheekbone.

A pent-up screech came from Mustang. "Stop — stop!" he gasped. "I'll tell yuh. We meant to drive yuh out, soon as we'd won!"

Long Lance comprehended enough English to understand the import of Mustang's words. He translated for the benefit of those among his people who did not know any language save the guttural Comanche. Sul-

179

len growls came from Indian throats.

"Who was it sniped some Comanches from ambush, to stir 'em up, Mustang?" demanded Hatfield.

When Mustang hesitated, Long Lance lowered a freshly heated iron toward his blinking, watering eyes. The big man quivered with terror, the sweat beads shining on his wrinkled, tortured forehead. He tried to hold out, to defy his captors.

"Sharpen some splinters to ram under his finger-nails, Long Lance," advised Hatfield, rolling a cigarette, lighting it with no show of emotion or pity.

Flowers waited, eyes yellow. Oak splinters six inches long, with needle points, were passed to the chief of the Comanches. Long Lance seized Mustang's right wrist and thrust one splinter up between the flesh and the nail.

"No — no!" screeched Flowers. "I'll tell — tell yuh anything." He began to blubber, all defiance gone from his quivering body.

"Answer then, who started the Indians off?" growled Hatfield.

"We did, some of us Snake Hats. We picked off a few Injuns to work 'em up against the settlers, so's they'd fall in with us. Fer Gawd's sake, Ranger, make that red devil quit! I'll do anything yuh say, if yuh'll

180

keep him from torturin' me any longer. I can't stand it."

Mustang Flowers was utterly broken. Words flowed from his thick lips, eyes rolling in terror every time Long Lance moved. The magnificent Indian chief stood, still holding the cooling iron, and there were more splinters lying at hand. The chief translated Flowers' confession into Comanche.

When they understood what the snake-band men had done, tricking them, intending to cheat them once they had used the Comanches, rage seized the braves. The leader of the young men who had rebelled against Long Lance's wise leadership, began to shout. "Torture this enemy to death," he cried. "Let us retreat out of Texas."

Approving yells rang out, but the Ranger put up his hand to address them. "Comanches," he told them gravely, "you have attacked innocent settlers of Texas and no matter where you go we will follow to avenge them. There is only one way for you to win our friendship, save yourselves. And in doing it you will be revenged on your enemies as well."

Hatfield's bold stand silenced them; uneasily the braves who had taken part in the raids eyed each other, watched the rugged

Lone Wolf.

"Later," Hatfield said slowly, "I will tell you what that way is. Now we will talk further with this prisoner."

He squatted again by Flowers. "Who's 'the guv'nor,' Mustang?"

Flowers gulped. Though cowed and beaten, fearing that slow torture that sent horrible pangs of anguish through his nervous system, he still hesitated. But as Hatfield frowned and turned toward the waiting Long Lance, Flowers said hurriedly:

"Jarvis — Granville Jarvis is his name."

"Where's he from?"

"Austin. He was throwed out last election, for stealin' state funds."

"Yeah. I heard of him though I never saw him. He killed a county sheriff who had him in custody when he escaped. Jarvis has his headquarters now in Making?"

Mustang nodded. Though he feared the Comanche torture, he was in even greater dread of the tall jigger who had bested him. But upon Hatfield he was forced to rely for life, since only the Ranger stood between Flowers and the avenging savages.

"If he learns I told," Flowers went on weakly, "he'll kill me. Yuh can't beat *him* fella. He's got ev'rything lined up, and rollin'. By the time yuh can get enough help

182

over here, Jarvis'll be in power, elected guv'nor of the new state of Jefferson. The citizens 're solid behind us."

Hatfield grunted. "Mebbe, on account of the crooked work yuh've laid on others! Who killed David Horton?"

"Jarvis."

"Why?"

"To keep Horton from makin' peace with Bell and his bunch, from provin' the sheepmen didn't kill them steers. Jarvis was at the B-in-a-Bell that night and he shot Horton from outside the winder."

"Huh. And tossed an empty shell inside the room to make it look like Bell done it and then reloaded. Only Lydie Bell picked it up and — Who sold that murder gun to Bell, to use at the match?" Hatfield fired the last question at Mustang.

"Ulman," came the answer. "Jarvis ordered him."

"Ulman, yore pard, who cleaned up on them hides from the pizened cows. Who blew up Making jail, and tried to feed me strychnine?"

"Jarvis wanted to finish yuh. Golon planted the pizen in the food, but it got the sheriff 'stead of you."

Singing Bear had squatted, motionless, the grizzly mask hiding his head and shoulders as he listened to Hatfield's quick translation of Mustang's confession.

In Comanche, Jim Hatfield said, "I need fighters I can depend on, Long Lance. There's one way to still the wrath of the white men, after what yore young braves have done. You know Virgil Tazewell, the trapper — he's with me in this. He's a friend."

Singing Bear grunted, pushed up the bear mask quickly. Hatfield saw his face for the first time. Singing Bear was very old, cheeks crisscrossed by myriad wrinkles. Only in the glowing, strong black eyes, sunk deep in his withered skull, did his intense life show.

Long Lance spoke to Hatfield: "Tazewell is a friend of the Indians. He was adopted into our tribe when he was a youth. He is Singing Bear's blood brother. Singing Bear would speak."

The Ranger did not understand why Long Lance stared at him so queerly. "I advise you to be careful of what you claim," the chief told him solemnly.

The old medicine man reached out a bony claw, and drew Jim Hatfield to him. "Come," he grunted.

Singing Bear would not allow anyone else to accompany them, as he led the Ranger, towering over the age-shrunken Indian, from the camp. On horseback, Hatfield went with the medicine man through the winding hills. Singing Bear escorted him to the cavern in the hillside, the spot where Long Lance had taken the Ranger to have his wound treated.

Bent double by years, Singing Bear led the way into the dark cave. At the Indian's order, Hatfield struck a match. Singing Bear was watching him closely, alertly. For an instant, the Ranger thought that the old fellow meant to attack him, for Singing Bear had a hand on his long knife.

"See," ordered Singing Bear.

The Ranger swung. In the yellow flare of the match, the dry walls of the cavern shone gloomily gray. Bundles of dried herbs, and food-stores, blankets, medicine masks, the possessions of Singing Bear, were strewn about.

But it was the man in the corner who held Hatfield's eyes. He sat propped on a pile of furs, legs covered by a bright blanket. His face was a skeleton's, yellow skin taut over the protruding bones. All the hair had been shaved from his head, the top of which was a horrible, burrowed scar, its edges jagged, the flesh discolored and thickly scabbed.

"Snake Hats do that," Singing Bear whispered hoarsely, as the match burnt the Ranger's fingers.

Hatfield struck another, aware that the medicine man was close to him, with the knife drawn. "I save — no one else knew, not even Long Lance! Now he lives. I know you, too, are an enemy of the Snake Hats!"

The lips of the man Singing Bear had snatched from the grave writhed as he groaned in pain. Hatfield, squatted before the weakened hombre in the depths of the medicine man's cave, watched the flickering, washed-out blue eyes open wide under Singing Bear's ministrations.

"Yeah," he muttered to himself, "he's smart, damn smart! I never guessed." And he told Singing Bear, "I am the sworn enemy of your enemies. I am going to smash the Snake Hats." After a time he asked, "Can he travel?"

Singing Bear shrugged, nodded, slipping the long knife back into its sheath.

The tall jigger rose, hitched up his gunbelt, heavy with the two blue-steel Colts and cartridges. He strode from the cavern, mounted the golden sorrel, and rode swiftly back to Long Lance's camp.

Mustang Flowers looked up at him fearfully. Sweat stood out on him, for Long Lance and his braves had taken advantage of the Ranger's absence to devil the prisoner further.

"So," Hatfield growled, "yuh didn't tell me the full truth, Flowers!"

"What — what is it?" gasped Mustang.

A sense of foreboding bore down on the tall Ranger. The terrible power of the enemy he was fighting to the last ditch was enough to make most men quail. Could he beat the foe, with his murderous cohorts, in this life-and-death game?

CHAPTER XIII
THE MEETING

It was Thursday night when the swift legs of the giant sorrel carried Jim Hatfield up to the Bell ranch-house. Outposts surrounding the place challenged him, letting him through when he was identified by B-in-a-Bell cowboys.

Armed men lounged in the yards, fetched in from the wide northwest by Marley Bell's messengers. Hundreds of horses were held in the corrals and on the wide sweep of grazing pastures close to the home ranch. Rifles and pistols, ammunition, glinted in the light from campfires. The ranchers had brought every man they could spare to the rendezvous ordered by their president, Marley Bell.

Bell came out to greet the tall Ranger. His face was tensely drawn, usually fiery eyes dull with a hopeless horror. It was plain that Bell was holding himself up by sheer nerve. Around his set lips showed a white circle.

"They got Lydie," he told Hatfield tonelessly. "Snatched her right from under my nose. And I figger they've snaffled Phil Horton, too. He started out to hunt her and he ain't come back." His hand was trembling as he thrust the threatening kidnap note into Hatfield's palm.

Hatfield read it quickly. Cold rage swept through him. His archenemy, Jarvis, seemed to anticipate every move that he made, counteracting it by a fresh atrocity.

"Yuh'll fight?" he drawled, facing Bell.

Marley shook his head. He was distressed. "Yuh see what it says: if we go to Making 'fore Saturday they'll kill her. I b'lieve they would do it. I sent some scouts toward town. They run into a ring of gunmen. Mebbe if I wait till Saturday, they'll let Lydie go without harmin' her."

"Bell," said Hatfield slowly, "the sidewinder yuh're up against is a liar, as well as a killer and thief. His name's Granville Jarvis and he's wanted for murder and thievery in Austin. He come to the Panhandle to take it over, split the territory from Texas. He had to smash yore association, since yuh're strong and would stick to Texas. He needed money to run his show, pay his imported gunmen; he's brought killers in from all over. He picked up some cash

189

sellin' them hides, and got more from forged leases and homestead titles placed by his crooked agents.

"He's got to stay hid, not let anyone know his true identity. If he wins tomorrer he won't let Lydie and Phil go, he couldn't, for they'd be witnesses against him. Savvyin' him as I do, I figger he'll hold 'em as hostages in case it comes to that. But if we charge in tonight, half-cocked, and fail to locate 'em, he'll break us 'fore we're ready. Callate if we hit fast enough we kin save 'em tomorrow."

Hatfield pitied the father, as he watched Bell struggling within himself. After a time he looked up into the strong face of the Ranger and his eyes lighted with some of their former fire. He thrust out his jaw.

"I'll fight," he said simply.

"Good. C'mon. I wanta talk to yore friends. We're facin' an army. That assembly's at three tomorrow afternoon and it's life or death for Texas."

"And us," muttered Bell.

He trailed the tall jigger, whose spurs jingled as he strode to the gathering. Horton's sheepmen, squatted near at hand, were off in a group of their own; though a truce existed, the cowmen and sheepherders could never live too close because of their

190

conflicting professions.

A tense quiet fell over the gathering, and calculating, shrewd eyes sized up the handsome, powerful Texas Ranger as he stood before the hard-bitten gun-fighters brought together by the Panhandle Grazers Association. These hombres were ready to defend their home range; for weeks they had pursued a chimera, hoping to avenge the ruin brought on them by the poisoning of their cattle, to find some order in the existing chaos. Once directed against the real enemy, Hatfield was aware that they would fight like demons.

He began to speak to them, and they fell under the spell of that soft yet compelling voice. When Hatfield finished, they knew who their enemeies were, and what part they must assume in the desperate battle that was approaching so swiftly.

It was still dark when Jim Hatfield, leading Jeff Smith, Olly Crouse and the tough sheepherders, with a contingent of fifty fighting cowboys, swung into Goldy's saddle and galloped across the moonlit plains toward Making City.

Forced to stake everything on the result of the next day's contest, he meant to win it or die for Texas.

There was a great deal to be done before

daylight came; disposals to be made, orders to be given, instructions that must be carried out, timed to the minute.

Death flapped black wings, hovering close over the Panhandle. . . .

Friday broke fair, a gentle breeze rustling the dry prairie grasses, rattling the cactus pods, stirring the fragrant blooms of the great plains.

Making City was already crowded with citizens from far and wide throughout Northwestern Texas, men whose faces were serious, worried with the gravity of the step they contemplated. There were also hundreds on hundreds of gunmen whose Stetsons were trimmed by a rattlesnake band dotted with a vermilion circle.

Delegates were still arriving from other counties, dusty gear showing the long miles they had ridden in answer to the call from the capital of the Panhandle. The plaza was filled with wagons and saddle horses; gamblers did a thriving business in the big saloons, roaring wide open, as men sought to forget for a moment the serious business at hand.

Every road into town was guarded by patrols of Snake Hats, hard-faced hombres with ready pistols who carefully inquired into the business of the incoming people.

192

Those who wore rattlesnake bands on their Stetsons were passed through with a short nod; often delegates from outlying sections were accompanied by members of the vast criminal-politico organization which had the northwest in its brutal grip.

At the north end of town, just beyond the last buildings, the large meeting field was being given the finishing touches. There was a wide, railed platform and wooden benches for delegates spread below, seats for a great number of citizens. Flags blew in the breeze, and carpenter hammers were pounding the last nails into the boards.

Beyond, in the distance, could be seen specks that were horsemen, sentinels sitting their saddles, watching the trouble, helping to check the arriving delegations. To the east, the prairie rose and fell in undulating waves. A deep gully, through which the scant rains would run, heavily fringed by mesquite and chaparral, extended east and west for several miles. Prairie dogs of the big villages that honeycombed the plains played in the sunshine, scampering in and out of the burrows.

By 2:30 the meeting ground was jammed with excited citizenry, delegates from every county of the Northwest, sent to this vital gathering to determine by vote the position of the territory. There was talk of the Comanche uprising, of the sheep-cattle war.

Way out on the plain, to the northeast, a dust cloud grew visible, rapidly approaching Making. Snake Hats, on the alert, watched its approach with ready guns.

Up on the wide platform, important delegates and citizens were being seated. John Farnsworth, the noble-browed orator, appeared to the accompaniment of cheers. He climbed the steps to the rostrum, his dignity great, his bearing assured. These men had heard his fiery speeches on his tour of the territory.

There were other speakers, Mayor Decker of Making, heads of other towns and communities involved. And in the growing crowd, men with rattlesnake bands on their Stetsons circulated, watching, listening.

In the distance, toward the northeast, a shot sounded, dimly. Signals passed in from the outposts, and from behind the buildings of Main Street appeared a compact body of riders, with rifles ready, heading out on the plain.

Two hundred Snake Hats were in the first bunch; another squadron, armed to the teeth, came in their drag, rolling across the flats toward the scene of trouble. Altogether, five hundred fighting men trotted forth, vigilant commanders riding the flanks to direct them.

A mile away they met a sentry, riding in hell-for-leather, one of the ring set around the city; others were retreating to join the main army of gunmen.

"It's that big jigger," the lookout reported. "He's got a tough gang of hombres with him!"

"Jest what we want," growled a hard-faced lieutenant. "C'mon, gents. We'll take care of him."

While at the assembly, as people turned to see what was going on behind them, out on the flats, John Farnsworth frowned, gave a quick signal to Mayor Decker of Making. Decker rose, a stout hombre with a florid face, clad in black frock-coat and tight-fitting dark trousers tucked into expensive boots.

"Fellow citizens of Northwest Texas," drawled Decker, "you know why we're here today. Lawlessness, Indian raids, have ruint us all. We got to take the responsibility for order into our own hands entirely. Victims have been shot down without mercy; the sheep-cattle war has crashed our banks. We must act!

"And now I take pleasure in introducin' to you John Farnsworth, the silver-tongued orator of the Panhandle!" Decker wiped the sweat from his hot brow with a large red bandanna, swept a hand toward Farnsworth, and sat down, relieved to be through with his speech.

Cheers rose as Farnsworth, white noble brow bared to the breeze, stood before them. He was an accomplished demagogue, well versed in the art of swaying the masses.

"I greet the delegates from the west," he began, "and from the south, from east and north. We are here to quell the Terror which has gripped our fair land. The violent men who have brought this chaos upon us, those feudal ranchers of the plains refuse to assist us. They must be crushed, along with the murderous redskins who have invaded our homes. We have appealed to Texas for aid —"

Farnsworth paused, the magic of his oratory holding them; his voice was resonant, impelling, reaching every listener. "But Texas has failed us!" he continued. "With full knowledge of the gravity of this step, I demand that we assume jurisdiction over our government. Secede! Let us form our own state organization, our own Rangers to restore order about us."

Farnsworth waited for his point to sink home then he began again. "If we secede our tax money will be used for our protection and needs instead of feeding into Austin which has left us gasping and prostrate, at the mercy of Comanches and the few bloodthirsty, selfish gunmen in our midst.

"Listen, even now you can hear the reports of their guns, as they try to force through to disperse this meeting. The lives of our children and ourselves are endangered by their bullets. We must act, act today, to prevent Federal intervention; shall it be said we cannot govern ourselves — ?"

As he paused, a cheer rose. Convinced of the dire emergency, the citizens of the Northwest were ready to vote for secession from Texas, to place their government in the hands of a criminal band.

Chapter XIV
The Battle

Two miles out on the plain Jim Hatfield rode at the head of his picked hundred, Horton's sheepmen, and chosen cattlemen. They carried their rifles full-loaded and ready. Jeff Smith and Olly Crouse marshaled their fighters at his left, while to his right came the ranchers.

Hell-for-leather, they rode to meet the multitude of Snakeband gunmen coming to meet them. Already bullets from the advance guard of the enemy whined evilly overhead, or spanked into the dirt, spurting up puffs of alkali dust.

"Line out," Hatfield ordered.

The band spread across a wide front, a space of several feet between horsemen. Hatfield opened up the return fire with his Winchester, and a Snake Hat left his saddle, was hit and pounded by swift flying hoofs of mustangs following, wild under their bits. Jeff Smith's buffalo gun roared defiance, the heavy slugs whooshing at the foe. The crack shots in Hatfield's band let go a volley that tore half a dozen leading gunmen out of the fray.

But it was five to one. Olly Crouse whooped in anguish threw up both stout arms; his horse galloped from the line, and as the sheepman's leg hold relaxed, he was thrown and dragged across the plain. Ranchers were hit, wounded or killed; Hatfield felt the singe of a slug along his ribs; others bit at his leather, and stung the golden sorrel.

"Swing!" he roared, voice audible above the blasting guns.

The enemy was rapidly massing on them, the volleys of leaden death like the drone of a tremendous machine.

Acting according to prearranged orders, the chosen force whirled, cutting away northwest, at an angle. The furious Snake Hats, belicving they were already victorious, set up howls of triumph, and, the taste of blood in their mouths, knowing they could overwhelm and kill every one of Hatfield's crowd, they pressed blindly, eagerly after.

Five hundred gunmen, drawn in by Jarvis from all over the northwest and the Panhandle, pounded hell-for-leather after the Ranger and his fighters.

Wind and dust stinging his drawn face as he zigzagged across the plain, Goldy skirting prairie dog holes with the expertness of a horse foaled on such ground, Hatfield swung in his saddle to shoot back at the oncoming Snake Hats. As he had been first in attack, he was last in retreat. He slowed for they were opening up, and he fired a last volley to bunch them again, those in the rear catching up, horses shouldering one another, snorting in the blazing excitement.

The calculating glance of the tall jigger swept the masses of the enemy. Men were going down on both sides; the hot battle brought hoarse shouts to pounding throats.

"We'll make it," Hatfield told himself.

They were close to that deep gully, fringed by heavy growths of snarled mesquite and other brush, some of it thirty feet high, starred with waxy white blooms. Four hundred yards behind, the Snake Hats rode, whooping for blood of which they were sure.

Then Hatfield's men, stopped by the ditch, threw themselves from their horses. Jeff Smith, his face a mass of blood where a bullet had ploughed, led his sheepmen, who flung themselves headlong into the gully. The ranchers followed, Hatfield leaving Goldy, the sorrel swinging to run along the line of bush.

"Now!" roared Hatfield, as he leaped down into the arroyo.

The ground the Snake Hats were passing seemed to rise, entirely leave the surrounding prairie. A tremendous explosion shattered the eardrums, and an enveloping cloud of dirt blotted out the enemy riders.

Two hundred Snake Hats were blown out of the battle by the dynamite Jim Hatfield had planted and drawn them over. Dirt, a hail of stones, rained down. The shattering reverberations of the explosion rattled across the plain. The wails of wounded men and torn horses shrieked on the warm air.

The remaining hundreds of Snake Hats collected their wits after the nerve-racking blow; leaders yelled harsh orders to their dazed men, drawing swiftly out of the smashed, uneven space. Then issuing from the deep gully, through the drifting clouds of smoke and dust, appeared a horde of naked Comanches, faces painted in vermilion patterns of war.

Winchesters, supplied by Snake Hat commissioners, glinted in the bronzed hands, as the Indians rode, bareback, pounding their wild mustangs into a wide, enveloping circle, war-whoops rising in a shrill, horrible threat.

Five hundred Comanches, led by Long

Lance and his sub-chiefs, whirled upon the stunned enemy; the Indians leaned on their horses, away from the Snake Hats, firing across the blanket used for a saddle or under the mount's neck. Thus a deadly hail of lead was poured into the enveloped army of gunmen.

Hatfield scrambled up the sliding gully bank, shrilled a whistle; Goldy trotted up to him, blood showing on his handsome flank, but the sorrel was only nicked. His red nostrils were wide in excitement as the Ranger leaped into his saddle. Jeff Smith, the survivors of the band, followed, running out to assist their Indian allies in crushing the main army of Snake Hats. The explosion of hundreds of guns, the shrill warcries of the Comanches, riding like the whirlwind, the screams of wounded, all made up a deafening din.

The Ranger raised a hand to Jeff Smith, and rode full-tilt east, out of the fray. Rounding the battlefield, he cut back toward Making City. The flying legs of the giant sorrel took him rapidly toward the town, sprawled out before him. He could see the black mass marking the meeting ground.

The Lone Wolf, knowing that the most important task lay before him, swung to the right, to circle and reach Making from the west side. Reinforcements, small bunches of men in the Rattlesnake hatbands, were rushing toward the battle that waged so furiously on the plain. It was fast turning into a massacre, for the hired gunmen, fighting only for money, stunned by the explosion and the unexpected appearance of the Comanches, were now concerned with saving their own hides.

Hatfield's Colts roared, cutting a path through the broken bunches of the enemy. A dozen recognized the tall jigger and swung after him, Goldy's extra speed keeping Hatfield out ahead of them.

As Hatfield swung around the buildings of Making, hotly pursued by the Snake Hats, with satisfaction he saw his own approaching reinforcements. So far his strategy was working with oiled precision.

Led by Marley Bell, a hundred and fifty members of the Panhandle Grazers, heavily armed, wcre speeding toward Making. And, guarded by a circle of horsemen, a small covered wagon rattled along at the rear of the cavalcade.

The dozen Snake Hats on Hatfield's trail suddenly saw the ranchers and their retainers. Sliding hoofs sent the disturbed dust high into the air as they pulled their horses up on haunches, turning to escape, but bullets rapped after them.

Marley Bell eagerly galloped up to the Ranger. "Have yuh seen her?" he cried.

Hatfield shook his head. "You go ahead. I can handle it now. She oughta be in that square brown house I told yuh of, or mebbe at the warehouse. Good luck. I'll join yuh as soon as I can."

Two dozen of his close associates at his heels, Bell detached himself from the main body, and cut through the line of houses.

Hatfield assumed command of the ranchers. He swung toward the meeting, up the lanes. Reaching Main Street north of the plaza, they saw a hundred Snake Hats drawn up across the road. Bullets from snipers in the houses began to sting among Hatfield's men.

With a war-whoop, the Ranger led the charge. Bullets rained upon them and men went down, bunched horses trampling them into the dust. The clash as the two lines of horsemen met head-on was loud; curses of fury, explosions of guns, ripped at the eardrums.

The Ranger was first through the blasted line of Snake Hats. Bleeding from his wounds, face blacked by dust and powder smoke, the tall jigger fired pointblank into the enemy, fighting at close range. The cattlemen never hesitated, never broke their formation as they charged, and they came through as the foe quailed, running for cover from those deadly guns.

"Bring up that wagon," commanded Hatfield.

The covered wagon was driven through Main, toward the assembly.

Alarmed citizens there looked around, wondering at the terrific burst of gunfire in Main Street. The densely packed crowd heard the bawled exhortations of John Farnsworth:

"Carry the word to your towns, your people! Sweep the Northwest. Split Texas. We will form our own proud Commonwealth of Jefferson, a new state with a new deal, a fresh bright star in the flag of the Union. I offer you your new governor, not a stranger to you but beloved and known throughout the whole of our territory. Virgil Tazewell, the famous trapper of Making, our capital city!"

Tazewell's lean figure rose from the seat on the rostrum and, as he faced the multitude, a tremendous ovation was offered him. Known far and wide as a square shooter, and a man devoted to the country, everybody loved the old trapper. His yellow beard, streaked with sliver, shone in the sunlight as he raised an arm for silence to speak.

"Delegates," he shouted, "the moment has come for us to act. I have loved Texas, but she has deserted us in our hour of need! We have formed our new state, Jefferson. Long may she live! I will lead you to peace and prosperity. I promise to crush the violent men who have brought ruin on us and to put down the Indian uprising, quickly and efficiently.

"And now, since you have chosen me, I know your people will respond to you and formally elect me. Even now we must fight to defend our state; the Comanches are close on us, and Marley Bell with his feudal retainers. There are rifles waiting and ready for you here, so you may protect yourselves against these bloodthirsty evildoers —" Tazewell broke off as a bullet whizzed over him. The milling throngs, those seated having leaped up, turned to see the tall Ranger, mounted on the giant golden sorrel, sweep toward the meeting.

Men with rattlesnake bands on their Stetsons edged from the outskirts of the crowd, guns appearing. Bullets whirled past the moving Hatfield as he rapidly galloped in, followed by Bell's ranchers.

Hatfield turned toward the platform, and

citizens opened a path before the big sorrel. Yells rang out and the people milled in confusion. The ranchers scattered to shoot it out with Sanke Hats who dared stand before them.

"Shoot that man!" Virgil Tazewell shouted, his eyes glowing fiercely, as he leaped to the front. "Citizens, he is a killer and a wanted criminal! Here, take these guns —" He indicated the open boxes of arms standing at the side of the platform.

Hatfield was close upon them, he leaped to the boxes from his saddle and, grasping the rail, vaulted it. His fist drove at Tazewell, knocked the trapper back; the lean hombre tripped and fell heavily, rolled under the rail.

Angry shouts rose from the citizens; here were a thousand honest men, fighters by inheritance; Tazewell was beloved throughout the country. To prevent a bloody riot that would end in the ranchers being wiped out by the deluded mob, Hatfield swept John Farnsworth and Mayor Decker, leaping to seize him from behind, out of his path and jumped to the front of the rostrum.

His powerful voice, rugged figure that held men's eyes, brought quiet enough so that he might be heard: "Men of the Northwest," he cried, "yuh've been flimflammed. A

207

murderer and a thief brought this great trouble on yuh. His agents laid the pizen that started the sheep-cattle war; his agents bribed the young men of the Comanche nation to raid the frontier. His name is Granville Jarvis and he's wanted for a killin' and embezzlement in Austin!"

"That jigger lies!" a Snake Hat screamed, and a bullet snapped through Hatfield's Stetson crown. One of Bell's men spurred his horse into the gunmen, knocked him senseless with a blow of his six-gun barrel.

The sweat poured off Hatfield's bronzed, grim face. He was making his great play to save Texas, prevent disintegration of the State. These people must be convinced that Texas considered them her children and offered them her full protection, that they had been hoodwinked by a venal organization of plotting criminals —

He reached in his pocket, drew forth the silver star set on a silver circle, emblem of the Texas Rangers, held it high so that everyone might see the badge as the sun glinted on it.

"My name's Jim Hatfield, folks," he told them, delegates from every county of the disaffected section. "I'm a Ranger, sent here to put down the trouble that's bin forced on yuh. I ain't askin' yuh to b'lieve jist my word, I have proof, full proof. Let that wagon through and listen, and yuh'll be convinced."

A commotion behind him forced him to turn; yells and shots rang out. Tazewell was already close to the outskirts of the crowd, which was enthralled by the Ranger's words; a compact bunch, his private bodyguard of Snakeband hombres, drove a path through for their leader.

Hatfield, looking over the heads of the people on the platform, heard the whistle of lead close over him. Tazewell's twisted, furious face was toward him as the trapper turned to shoot. Several of the ranchers spurred toward the bunch. Bullets rapped into the horses, into men's bodies, and for a moment there was a fierce, sharp struggle. Out of the melee Tazewell's tall figure broke, ran behind the near buildings, where horses waited.

Skeptical eyes were upon the Ranger. The tide was standing still now, ready to surge one way or the other — he dared not leave.

CHAPTER XV
THE TRAIL ENDS

The covered wagon, the one Hatfield and Phil Horton had used to spirit Mustang Flowers out of Making, was close upon the platform. From it Bell's men lifted two figures.

One was the giant gunman, Mustang Flowers. He was unsteady on his feet, and he licked his swollen lips, watered eyes blinking in the bright light. Brown scars showed on his cheeks, marks of the hot Indian irons. He glanced at the Ranger, whom he feared.

"Yuh all know Mustang Flowers," Hatfield announced. "He's got a few words to say to yuh. He was a charter member of that crooked bunch I spoke of, but he's reformed."

Mustang gripped the railing with both big hands, licked his dry, cracked lips. Silence fell. "Friends," Flowers began shakily, "I gotta admit to some mean tricks. We done pizened the range and started the sheep-cattle war up here, to bust the Panhandle and Northwest away from Texas. We hadda smash Bell's strong bunch 'fore we could take over. I done it all by Jarvis' order —" he broke off.

"Go on," Hatfield ordered sternly.

"Jarvis murdered David Horton, the sheepman. Shot him through the winder at the ranch, so's it'd seem Bell done it and purvent any truce."

Murmurs of rage rose from the crowd. Hatfield signaled the men at the wagon and a thin figure, a terrible scar visible on his shaved pate, was lifted to the platform.

"Yuh all know Virgil Tazewell," cried Hatfield. "Well, here he is. This is the real Tazewell. The hombre who stood up here, claimin' to be Tazewell, whom yuh meant to elect guv'nor of yore new state, is Granville Jarvis, killer and thief. He's a master at disguise and, lookin' much like the trapper, he done took his place.

"The real Tazewell was trappin' in the western hills. He's a close friend of the Comanches, blood brother to Singing Bear, their medicine man. Tazewell advised the Injuns not to go on the war-path, not to listen to the Snake Hats. When he started home to Making, he was dry-gulched, the

211

top of his head most blowed off.

"Jarvis, rigged up in the same getup, clothes stole from Tazewell, beard dyed and cut like Tazewell's, rode in and took the trapper's place. But Singing Bear, the Comanche medicine man, managed to save the real Tazewell, treated him and kept him hid. The Comanches have helped Texas and you; they're off the war-path, the sheep-cattle war's settled, and the Snake Hats busted."

The still weak Virgil Tazewell, held up by willing hands, raised a hand in salute. Now the spellbound audience stood in awed silence for a moment.

"Three cheers for Texas!" a man shouted, then leaped high.

A mighty roar of approbation shattered the warm air. The tide had turned for Texas. With deep relief, Jim Hatfield realized he had saved his glorious state.

The Lone Wolf slipped from the rostrum, remounted Goldy, and, breaking from the crowd, cut up Main Street. The Comanches, Jeff Davis and his hombres, had smashed and defeated the killers on the plain; those Snakeband gunmen remaining were riding hell-for-leather in every direction, escaping while they might.

He heard firing at the south end, distant

yells of fighting men. As he galloped full-speed down the cluttered road, the magnificent sorrel cutting in and out of the excited groups of people, he saw before him a dozen dusty hombres coming toward him. He whirled up to them. It was Lieutenant Jack Carney, of the Texas Rangers, leading the troop promised by McDowell.

"Howdy, Jim," grunted Carney. He was a lean young man, a good officer and a hard fighter. "We had some trouble gettin' through, and jest made it. A bunch of gunmen blocked us off and we hadda shoot a hole. Lost a couple privates, too!"

"I can use yuh, there's plenty cleanin' up to be done," Hatfield told him. "Arrest any hombre yuh see wearin' a rattlesnake hatband with a vermilion circle dottin' it. C'mon, I'm after the ringleader of the gang."

He swung toward the square brown house, that had been Jarvis' headquarters for the Making district. Dismounting, he saw Marley Bell lying at the door, Stetson knocked off, a bloody bullet gash in his scalp. The boss of the Panhandle Grazers had taken a slug that had knocked him out. Four of his selected group of fighters were heaped around him.

Hatfield gave an order, and a Ranger bent

213

over Bell to pick him up and carry him to first-aid. The Lone Wolf smashed into the door.

The place was deserted. He ran on out, and remounting, Carney and his men following, headed for the south end, toward the warehouses. Smoke was pouring from Tazewell's big building. The shots he had heard had come from there; more of Bell's contingent, assigned to rescue Lydie and Horton, lay in the warehouse yard, around several Snake Hats they had taken with them.

In the distance, across the plain to the southwest, Hatfield could see a body of riders retreating; while hanging on their flanks, whirled the remnants of Marley Bell's gunfighters.

He touched spurs to the golden sorrel; Goldy flew toward the scene. As he came up, a Bell cowboy, blood streaming down his face, eyes wild with fury, raced up. "They got Lydie and that sheepman," he bawled. "They're holdin' 'em up so's we can't shoot into 'em!"

The Lone Wolf's gray-green eyes rapidly took in the situation. There were about fifty men, rattlesnake bands on their Stetsons, in that crew, the remnants of Jarvis' broken army.

Hatfield searched eagerly for the tall, lean arch-foe, Granville Jarvis, whose cunning, murderous brain had devised the catastrophe that had overwhelmed the Northwest. But the crowd of gunmen was well-bunched; one rode with the slight figure of Lydie Bell held before him, and Phil Horton was tied to the saddle of a led horse. Whichever way the Bell men tried to attack, the helpless captives were thrown out so that the cowmen must kill their friends if they fired.

Carney was up with his Rangers, every man a tried and true soldier, ready to die for Texas.

"Circle," ordered Hatfield briefly.

They galloped in a wide arc, Goldy flashing out to head off the advance of the Snakeband gunmen, who began firing at the Rangers and the few Bell punchers who remained.

Led by the Lone Wolf, the contingent of Rangers coolly ignored the hot lead; two or three received wounds, and one died as he rode, but they formed a ring that stopped the retreat.

Jim Hatfield, blue-steel Colt in hand, spurred Goldy straight into the mob. Bullets cut his flesh and clothes, bit the sorrel, but with Carney and his troopers, they closed upon the furious enemy. Carefully picking their targets, avoiding the girl and Horton, shoved out toward them, a number of the Rangers reached the cursing, shooting foe.

Hand-to-hand fighting ensued; pointblank the deadly Ranger guns roared into the traitors of the Panhandle. In the thick of the fray Jim Hatfield rushed up to the spot where Lydie Bell was held; she was conscious, her amber eyes wide with mute appeal. Horton, trussed, gagged, watched with fresh hope as he recognized his tall friend, whirling in.

The Rangers never faltered; coolly they followed Hatfield's example, and the skirmish was brief. As the appalled Snakeband gunmen, awed by the terrific fighting men upon them, threw away their weapons in surrender, Jim Hatfield clipped the hombre holding Lydie, and the man slumped in his saddle. Pushing Goldy against the dancing mustang, Hatfield snatched Lydie Bell to the safety of his arms.

Phil Horton was quickly released, but he was so stiff he could scarcely move. "Jim!" he cried to Hatfield. "Tazewell, he's crooked, he cheated you. His men kidnaped Lydie, knocked me over when I went to the warehouse. I recognized him later on; he tried to torture me into telling where Mustang and you were, but I lied and managed to convince him I didn't know much!"

Squatted beside Horton, Lydie propped there, grateful for rescue, Hatfield nodded, asked, "Where's Tazewell, Jarvis is his real name?"

"Over there!" Phil Horton raised an arm, pointing west. Hatfield looked, and, far out on the plain, observed a dust cloud rapidly receding. "He deserted his bunch and lit out alone," Horton said.

"Figgered this gang'd draw me," muttered the Lone Wolf.

He rose up, mounted Goldy. Carney came over. "Want me, Jim?"

Jim Hatfield's rugged face was bleak. "No. Stay here and look out for these prisoners, Carney. I'll be back."

The golden sorrel lined out, full-speed, after the fleeing Jarvis.

The wind whistled past the tall rider's ears as he grimly sought to overtake his archenemy. Mile after mile, the plain spread behind him, Making growing to a spot in the distance. In the sky showed the black clouds of buzzards, dropping over the north of town.

Hatfield was gaining on Jarvis. He could make out the yellow bearded face as the

217

man ahead turned to look behind, to see the Ranger, hot after him.

As the giant sorrel pounded madly on the trail, skirting the gopher holes, and running lightly, feeling a way across the prairie-dog villages, Hatfield checked his Colts, made certain they were full-loaded. The chin-strap of his Stetson was drawn tight, bunching up his jutting jaw.

Jarvis, seeing he could not hope to outdistance his pursuer, turned, dismounted and quickly unshipped a rifle. The sunlight glinted upon its shining barrel as the arch-criminal lay flat on the plain to fire at the oncoming Ranger.

Off to the north, a fresh dust-cloud rolled, but Jim Hatfield was intent on his foe. He heard the close bullet that shrieked within a foot of his moving head. The blue-steel Colt rose to reply, but the range was long, the sorrel moving full-speed over uneven footing. A dust spurt behind Jarvis' prostrate figure showed he had missed.

Never faltering, Hatfield spurred Goldy on. Then a long rifle bullet struck him in the right shoulder; he felt the sickening impact, and was knocked half out of his saddle. As his right arm fell helpless at his side, Goldy swerved to avoid a pitted section of earth; the movement, with the iron thighs relaxed from the shock of his wound, sent the Ranger slipping. He did not fight to hold on but let himself go, rolling over and over on the dusty ground.

The pain of the shattered shoulder kept his teeth gritted, as he lost momentum, another bullet from Jarvis ripping the cloth of his shirt. He drew the Colt from his left holster, and coolly took aim, steady upon the solid earth. A hundred yards from Jarvis, snuggled against the dirt, he raised his thumb from the hammer spur and the blue-steel pistol spoke.

Jarvis lay still. His rifle did not speak again. Wary of a trap, yet eager to reach his enemy, Hatfield began to crawl inch by inch toward him, hampered by his paralyzed right side.

He could see the twisted face of the tall man clearly now, and there was a bloody gash in Jarvis' cheek — suddenly the hombre rose up with a shriek, sent a shot at the crippled Lone Wolf.

Hatfield fired in the echoes of Jarvis' gun. The final slug from his foe had ranged into his leg, cutting the flesh as it tore on through his boot. Jarvis, on his knees, threw up both hands, the rifle flying from his grip. He fell on his back, arched in spasmodic agony, writhed a moment, then lay still.

Through blurred eyes, the Ranger lay, watching, unable to move for a moment. From the north, the approaching dust-cloud resolved itself into Chief Long Lance, with a large band of his victorious Comanches.

Long Lance whirled up on his magnificent buckskin, threw himself off the mustang's back, ran to Jarvis and stooped over the dead figure. Something flashed in the sunlight.

Jim Hatfield, pulling himself together, began to crawl toward Jarvis; several of Long Lance's braves, coming up, recognized him, lifted him and carried him to their chief.

Jarvis lay, a bullet hole in the center of his forehead, Hatfield's last shot. The dyed yellow beard, half off — spirit gum loosed by the heat — stirred in the breeze across the prairie.

As Hatfield, supported by Comanches, staggered up, hopping on his uninjured leg, Chief Long Lance uttered a loud warwhoop of victory, waving to the sky the scalp of the arch-impostor Granville Jarvis . . .

Twenty-four hours later, wounds bandaged, painfully stiff, Hatfield and Goldy headed south. In spite of his injuries the Texas

220

Ranger led Lieutenant Carney and his hard-bitten men on a clean-up campaign. They rode for several days, pausing at every town and settlement to arrest, and lodge in the local jails, all gunmen caught with rattlesnake hatbands, the mark of the deadly society which had overrun Northwest Texas.

They garnered fifty more prisoners; others fled before their approach. The main body of the gang had been in Making, smashed by Hatfield's forces. Too, the delegates were returning from Making, with the news of what had occurred; that peace had come.

Finishing the clean-up, leaving final details to the efficient Carney and his men, Jim Hatfield swung back to Making City. There were adjustments to be made there. Jarvis' funds had been seized, and some repayment would be attempted to those who had lost so heavily through his machinations. . . .

Captain McDowell greeted his star Ranger with a hearty handshake, gripping his left hand, for the Ranger's right shoulder was in a sling and he limped heavily as he walked.

McDonald led him inside and pushed the whiskey bottle and cigars toward the Lone Wolf.

"Yuh've shore earned 'em, Jim," McDowell cried. "Thanks to you, the Northwest's quiet. Jest had a wire from Carney everything's settled down and they're grateful to Texas and the Rangers. No danger now of Federal intervention. This here Granville Jarvis was right cunnin', at that!"

Hatfield nodded. He still bore the wounds inflicted upon him by his arch-enemy, and it would be a long time before the stricken Northwest forgot Granville Jarvis.

"So Jarvis figured on bein' guv'nor of a new state, him bein' sore at Texas for throwin' him out."

"Yessir. He was built a good deal like Virgil Tazewell and fixed hisself up so he was a spittin' image of the trapper, who's a favorite up there."

"But Jarvis won't try splittin' any more states, will he?"

The Ranger's headshake was grim. "He was dead 'fore I left, Cap'n. Took me time to hit the right trail, for from yore say-so, I knowed Tazewell must be okay, and a true friend. On'y it wasn't Tazewell I contacted, but Jarvis in disguise, so he savvied ev'ry move I meant to make ahead of time. He was one smart sidewinder."

McDowell laughed and the inkwell danced as he banged his gnarled fist on the desk. "But he run into someone a danged sight smarter, someone who saved Texas!"

Later McDowell stood outside watching

as Jim Hatfield, terror of lawbreakers in the Lone Star State, mounted the golden sorrel and headed Goldy into the ruby halo of the setting sun.

The light from the window fell on the fighting line of the Lone Wolf's set jaw.

While Hatfield lived, so would Texas live.

We hope you have enjoyed this Large Print book. Other Thorndike, Wheeler, Kennebec, and Chivers Press Large Print books are available at your library or directly from the publishers.

For information about current and upcoming titles, please call or write, without obligation, to:

Publisher
Thorndike Press
295 Kennedy Memorial Drive
Waterville, ME 04901
Tel. (800) 223-1244

or visit our Web site at:

http://gale.cengage.com/thorndike

OR

Chivers Large Print
published by BBC Audiobooks Ltd
St James House, The Square
Lower Bristol Road
Bath BA2 3SB
England
Tel. +44(0) 800 136919
email: bbcaudiobooks@bbc.co.uk
www.bbcaudiobooks.co.uk

All our Large Print titles are designed for easy reading, and all our books are made to last.